WARRIOR'S VOW

WARRIORS OF YEDAHN #2

A SORA STARGAZER ROMANCE

EMMA ALISYN

HARD CANDIES PUBLISHING

Copyright © 2016 by **Emma Alisyn**

All rights reserved. No part of this publication may be reproduced, distributed or transmitted in any form or by any means, without prior written permission.

Hard Candies Publishing

Publisher's Note: This is a work of fiction. Names, characters, places, and incidents are a product of the author's imagination. Locales and public names are sometimes used for atmospheric purposes. Any resemblance to actual people, living or dead, or to businesses, companies, events, institutions, or locales is completely coincidental.

Cover Design by Emma Alisyn
Editing by Michelle Hoffman

Warrior's Vow/Emma Alisyn. – 1st ed.
Print Edition ISBN 978-1545437414
Kindle Edition ASIN B01LK2V5D2

ACKNOWLEDGEMENTS

Thank you to the Fiercely Real Readers who gave valuable time to help shape this story into a spicy, as error free as possible, read. I am so grateful for your effort and input.

B.J. DeFilippo
Tiffani Rippy
Jessie Haynes
Sayyidah Ali

SORA STARGAZER TITLES

WARRIORS OF YEDAHN SERIES
WARRIOR'S BOND #1
WARRIOR'S VOW #2
WARRIOR'S MATE #3
WARRIOR'S REIGN #4

ARCHANS OF AILAUT SERIES
WARRIOR AWAKENING #1
WARRIOR ENFLAMED #2
WARRIOR AVENGED #3

CONTENTS

1 8
2 28
3 41
4 56
5 71
6 84
7 97
8 114
9 129
10 144
EPILOGUE 152
WARRIOR'S MATE 156
ABOUT THE AUTHOR *175*

1

Some days just sucked.

Well, if she was honest- which she always was because who had the energy to lie to the woman in the mirror- *most* days just sucked.

Months.

Years.

Hell... *life.*

The sparring pair she'd tumbled into rose from the ground, curses sprinkling the air like fairy dust. Resentment welled as she pushed to her feet, locking her jaw from the effort even a simple move took. They were all beginners- they should expect a few... mishaps. The Third Form wasn't exactly easy. All those waving arms and legs.

WARRIOR'S VOW

Head spinning, Mila bent, bracing her hands on her knees until her blackening vision cleared. It wasn't especially hot outside today, but she had other issues.

"Trainee."

Other issues included the Adekhan assigned to her training unit. He hated her guts. Or at least did a swell job of imitating someone who hated her guts.

"Clumsy as usual."

Her lips thinned. No use explaining- anything she said would only look like whining. They knew her issues. She'd disclosed everything in her application, if he'd bothered to read it, which wasn't likely. Only God knew why they'd approved her, but the brochure said the Yadeshi didn't give a flying fig about health problems. Maybe the rumors about their advanced medicine weren't rumors, but if so she hadn't been singled out for any special treatment yet.

Well, that wasn't quite true, but did the healing sessions with Jaron count? Yeah, she'd realized a few weeks after first meeting him- having been sent to the infirmary after passing out- that the glowy tattoo thingy was reserved just for her. She still didn't know why it was reserved just for her. It was good it was, cause Mila didn't like the idea of him taking off his shirt and pressing his chest against any woman but her.

"Trainee."

Mila realized she was mentally babbling and grimaced, bringing her mind back to present time and the teacher standing in front of her. His methods left somewhat to be desired since even with humans, calling a student clumsy wasn't considered the most productive teaching method.

Mila straightened when her head was clear. Adekhan Ithann stood, arms crossed over his chest, blue eyes... well... icy. Could alien blue eyes be anything *but* icy? Even Jaron's eyes, so deep a blue they were nearly black, were rarely anything resembling warm. Despite months of inexplicable friendship. Despite the occasional flashes of something across his face when she caught him looking at her lately.

"Apologies," she said. "I'll do better."

"I doubt if you are able to do better."

"No such thing as a bad student- only a bad teacher."

Mila winced as soon as the words left her mouth. That bit of disrespect would earn her an extra three laps- and her body just couldn't take it. No choice but to take it- couldn't afford to get kicked out.

"Mila, you okay?"

Gayle's voice and the sound of jogging feet approaching. Her best friend skidded to a halt, the beaded tips of her long blue braids smacking Mila in the back. No health problems there- the woman was the picture of tall, athletic, High Tier strength. Glowing golden brown skin and snapping dark eyes, now subdued from concern. She was the only person who knew the real deal- but her mouth was sworn to stay shut.

"I'm good."

"Girl, you don't look good. You need to go sit down."

Mila glared at her. "I'm *good.*"

Gayle rolled her eyes and looked at Ithann, expression tightening to something she would probably think imitated politeness. "Can we take a break?"

He snorted. "Take her to the medic to have the bleeding tended."

Both women froze. Mila looked down at herself, noticing the streaks of blood on her bare knees for the first time. Triple damn.

"Oh, fuck," Gayle said.

The Adekhan frowned. "If this is how Earth women respond to scrapes-"

Gayle snarled something in the language of her homeland. Mila kept her face straight as the Adekhan scowled at her. She knew at least a dozen curse words in that dialect. None of them benign.

Mirth faded as her nerve endings belatedly fired. Gayle grabbed her shoulder. "Come on, let's get you to Jaron."

"Drop her off and return right away," Ithann called.

* * *

There were a handful of other students in the medic's office. Serious injuries would be treated at the local hospital, but anything short of punctured organs or shattered bones, Jaron and his staff could handle.

"Get Jaron," Gayle told Jaron's medical assistant. "It's an emergency."

Mila dropped onto a bench, staring down at the steadily seeping wounds on her knees. Never should have left the house without her skin covered. She knew better- but she'd been so tired last night and hadn't done laundry and damned if she'd come to training in smelly gear. She might be piss poor, but she didn't have to stink.

And the one day her skin was bare to the elements, she just had to take advantage.

The assistant, Stacia, eyed Mila. "I don't think-"

If Stacia had been Yadeshi, Gayle probably wouldn't have leaned over the desk and grabbed the woman's arm, shaking her. "Get *Jaron!*"

Great. But Mila didn't have the breath to tell Gayle to calm down. Instead, she reached out mentally and gave Stacia a... nudge. When she felt the woman's resistance fade, Mila pulled her mind back inside her skull where it belonged. Besides, too much influencing and she'd have a headache for days.

A door down the hallway opened, a tall- well, they were all tall, and blue, and pretty damn hot- Yadeshi male in their typical non training uniform of a sleeveless wrap shirt and loose trousers emerged. He wore a white lab coat over his clothing, more for the benefit of the humans since Mila gathered Yadeshi doctors wore something different on their own planet.

Jaron crossed the hall in record time, moving in that fast but not seemingly fast way they all moved. Just... ground eating strides that managed to look casual.

"What happened?" Jaron demanded, expression shading from doctor pleasant to warrior-just-waiting-for-an-excuse-to-fight-something. He scooped her up, overkill, but then Jaron rarely *asked* when it came to her treatment. "Stacia, log Mila."

He ate more ground, Gayle on his heels. Mila listened to his heart beat, the pace slower than a human's at resting rate. His cool tenor deepened to something closer to baritone with her ear on his chest. Jaron glanced at her friend as he kicked open the exam room door and set Mila on the paper covered table.

"You need to return to training, Gayle."

Gayle crossed her arms, legs spread in a Form Mila recognized as Stubborn.

"I'll be fine," Mila said, lying down and closing her eyes. "Go before Ithann makes you do laps."

"Adekhan Ithann," Jaron corrected.

With her eyes closed she heard Gayle sigh and the door clicked shut, Jaron rummaging through drawers. A crinkle of simple paper packets.

"What happened?" he asked.

Her eyes remained closed, though her thighs tensed at the first touch of cool fingers on her bloodied knees.

"Fell training. Third Form."

"You tripped on the Third Form?"

She would have grit her teeth from the sigh in his voice, but didn't have the energy.

"How is your energy level today?"

"Same."

He cleaned her knees, paused. "Mila- why isn't your blood clotting?"

The reason why she'd panicked at the simple scrape. "It will, it'll just take longer than normal."

"You can't afford longer than normal." His tone cooled considerably. "Mila. Why is your blood not clotting?"

She sighed, opening her eyes, and sat up. A hand on her thigh kept her from swinging down from the table. Mila glared at him, though her anger didn't even cause him to blink. In her current condition, even a child could keep her held down.

"You know I'm sick."

"I know what you've told me."

He stared her down, tension humming between them. Over the months of their friendship, she'd explained as much as she had to, and no more. He didn't press- but he watched her like a hawk. Or a scientist, figuring out a puzzle. Usually she ignored him because the benefits of his friendship outweighed the annoyance of him constantly examining her.

"Well, I'm sicker now."

His eyes narrowed. Mila tensed. Sometimes... she thought the calm, sardonic facade was a veneer for... something else. When they'd first met, even after the first few weeks of casual companionship, she'd figured he was like her. A bit of a loner, a bit of a geek. He wore his hair shorter than the warriors, tousled and messy around his ears, and his frame was leaner. He wasn't nearly as abrupt and controlling as an Adekhan. But... lately it seemed the leash on his good behavior was slipping.

It was as if he'd begun to take her illness personally.

"I think you're lying to me, Mila," he said. Voice low, and pleasant. "I thought we had an understanding."

She watched as he scooted towards the cabinet on his wheeled stool. He withdrew additional supplies and returned to his position- but she hadn't moved, despite the opportunity.

"Look- there's no reason to whine about what's going on with me," she said.

Jaron smiled, but it wasn't pleasant. "I'm your primary physician. That's how humans say it? You should whine." He paused. "You asked me not to look at your medical records. Am I going to regret that indulgence?"

She hadn't wanted to be treated like the poor, sick trainee. And later, when they'd started to become friends and he realized he needed to see her charts, she hadn't wanted to endure his pity. Mila crossed her arms, channeling Gayle. Except she kept her mouth shut, which so *wasn't* Gayle. He watched her with the focus of a snake about to strike while he tended her knees.

"This is a second skin treated with some antibiotics," Jaron said. "It will help you clot, and speed your healing."

"Thanks."

He put away his supplies and she edged off the table.

"Be still."

The chill command froze her muscles. "Look, Jaron-"

He was next to her in a second, at full height looking down, a hand resting on the table close to her hip. Nothing overtly intimidating about his posture. That was Jaron- he would consider overt to be beneath him.

"Why isn't your blood clotting, Mila?"

Fuck. The utter reasonableness of his tone was a mask, and told her exactly what Gayle's Form Stubborn did. He wasn't going to let her budge until she opened her mouth.

"It's a side effect," she said, shoulders slumping.

His fingers thrummed on the table. "Of what, Mila?"

"You know, this 'Mila' shit is going to drive me crazy. My own mother doesn't say my name in that tone."

"Your mother is-" he stopped himself, mouth tightening.

She looked down at the beige tiled floor. Bland, too clean, the faint scent of industrial lemon disinfectant. The same floors of every hospital and institution she'd been in and out of with her mother since she was old enough to walk. They'd had long talks about her mother, about her upbringing. She'd revealed things to him she'd never told anyone, and he'd taken her secrets and... kept them safe. Not judged.

Fingers under her chin, gently forcing her face up. "Tell me."

She flinched from the gentle lash of his tone, implacable no matter how soft and falsely civilized. She didn't much like this side of him- the bossy side.

"I- signed up for a research program."

He examined her face, not responding right away. "Do you mean a clinical trial? Experimental medication?"

"Yes."

"Why would you do that? I've told you about the clinical trials at the facilities in this city."

He had. As a medical resident at the local university hospital when he wasn't in this YETI medical office, he'd shared quite a few stories with her about the health care system he'd come to Earth to learn. Amusing and grim.

She slid off the table, jerking her head away. "None of your business, Jaron."

He moved, casually. Subtly blocking the door. She didn't quite have the nerve to push past him- she didn't want to confront the snake under his eyes. The patient predator ready to pounce and bite- the one he pretended didn't exist when they spent hours watching her old flat screen television or sitting in a used bookstore- the kind without coffee so she didn't have to be embarrassed from not being able to afford a cup.

"I thought I was your friend," he said. "Like Gayle."

Was he insane? Like *Gayle?* Gayle wasn't a big, blue, deadly, sexy... whoops. No business thinking *sexy*. Even if her body was strong enough to endure sex with a Yadeshi warrior- and she heard the bedroom to them was as much a battle field as the training circles- it wasn't like she was stupid enough to think he wanted that from her. She'd been pretty once, when she'd been healthy. Curvy.

That was a long time ago.

"I guess." She shrugged, hating that the movement felt despondent.

"Does Gayle know?"

She said nothing.

"I see. You don't trust me. I didn't realize I'd caused you distress, Mila. Perhaps I should leave you alone for a while."

The manipulative bastard. He *knew* he was her only friend besides Gayle. He was blackmailing her.

She exhaled noisily. "You're a jerk. They're paying me. I'm broke, alright?" No other way to tell him, except the stark, cold truth. "I didn't want to tell you because I didn't want you to bitch."

"So you would sacrifice your health for *money?*"

She'd rarely seen him angry- well, never. But despite the level tone, she knew he was angry now. The air around him crackled, a sudden shift from patient and predatory to growly and predatory. Snake? Nah. More like a giant tiger.

Mila glared. He had no right to judge her. None. Let him face what she was facing and then come talk to her. "I'm dying and it doesn't matter if they experiment with me- they pay."

He took a step back, head snapping as if she'd punched him a good one under the jaw. "*What?*"

Ah, shizzle. "I mean- I meant-"

No way to influence him to forget those words. She'd never tried her little trick on a Yadeshi. The hard look on his face warned her to *never* try it with him.

Besides, she had the suspicion that being around him was what enhanced her ability anyway.

"I know you need money," he said. "I was waiting for you to come to *me.*"

Her mouth opened, closed. "Why in the hell would I do that? You aren't my man."

"You don't even know what that means." He paused, visibly calmed himself. If calm meant his expression hardening from hot anger to cold determination. "Whatever you need, you come to me, Mila. Money, healing... anything you need."

Mila shook her head. "But why? I don't understand."

"Do you think I'm healing you for nothing? Do you think sharing myself with you is *routine?*" He stared at her, nostrils flaring just enough to let her know he was struggling with temper.

Her own anger rose. "You still haven't answered why! Why be my friend, why heal me, why..." she faltered. He was acting like a lover, not a friend, a doctor.

"Because you trust me. Because I can. Because I already failed once."

She stared at him. "Who? Who did you fail?"

He shook his head, holding out a hand, fingers curling as if to draw in her essence. "And because, Mila, when you are fully healed, at full strength, I plan to collect on the debt."

The word collect had never sounded so full of dark intent, sensual promise. The place between her thighs tingled the way it did when his voice deepened in a certain way- as if he was teasing her. He inhaled and Mila blushed. She knew Yadeshi had excellent senses.

His eyes gleamed. "Promise me, Mila. You will come to me."

"I... for healing only. Not for money. No! Don't protest. I have some dignity left. I'm not going to be your poor sick friend."

"If not now, Mila, then soon. It's only a matter of time." He closed the gap between them, hands on her arms. "Take off your shirt."

She knew what he wanted and shook her head. "No, Jaron. I appreciate it, but it isn't helping and-" she faltered.

And she had the feeling these little sessions had somehow caused the spike in her ability. Before him, she'd never been able to nudge people as easily as she could now.

Keen eyes, an almost black sapphire, pinned her. "And what? You said 'for healing, Jaron.' Was that a lie?" His hands slid down her arms, under her shirt and skimmed her ribs.

She swore. "Damnit. No, it wasn't a lie."

But it only made things worse. Every time he did the glowy thing with his tattoos, she felt better for a while. But she also felt desire she had no business feeling. Like now, with his hands searing her bare skin.

"Mila," he whispered, head lowering.

She tensed, eyes caught in the web of his gaze. How many times had she imagined his lips on hers, imagined that he returned even a portion of her desire?

Lower, lips almost...

A brisk knock on the door.

"You have patients," she said, jerking away.

A long moment of strained silence, his eyes warning her she'd just barely escaped. "We'll talk about this tonight. Promise me no more experimental drugs."

"No."

His hands tightened. Not hurting her- he was a doctor. He wouldn't hurt her. "I can *make* you promise."

"And how would you do that?"

Jaron's smile was knowing. "You know how. And you've accepted my healing before. That means something to the Yadeshi. It gives me... leeway with you."

She put her hands against his chest and pushed. He didn't budge. "Let me go, Jaron! I'm tired, I don't want to argue about this."

It wasn't an excuse, she *was* tired. Exhausted. And didn't want to think about the subtle shift in their comfortable relationship happening; she wanted the shift to stop so she could think, readjust. He was more dangerous than she'd thought- not the affable, platonic alien. Which meant she had to get out of here, and now.

Another, more insistent knock, saved her.

"We'll talk about this tonight, Mila," he said, releasing her.

She pushed past him, deliberately bumping his side. When her hand turned the doorknob, he said, "Be home. You don't want me to chase you down."

She believed him.

2

Jaron gave his patients the necessary amount of attention and no more. After sending the last human on her way- a teenager with a badly sprained wrist- he left the office.

He didn't remove his lab coat- it served as a kind of invisibility shield. The warriors weren't entirely bright sometimes, especially the ones sent to Earth to mate human women. No one wanted to waste the best seed on humans, at least not until the offspring proved normal enough. The first batch of children were barely even out of primary levels- too early for anyone to tell if they were defective.

Cross breeding was always problematic.

Stepping into the indoor training arena, he scanned the mats for Ithann. An Adekhan. Jaron contained a snort. They'd make anyone an Adekhan these days. The man's voice, barking at a female student, drew Jaron's attention. He picked his way through the training groups, some as young as a decade, giving Adekhan Benyon a nod.

Jaron's gaze caught on Benyon's human mate for a moment. A lucky match, and the Adekhan had leave to take his new family home to Yadesh within the week. Proof that Jaron's... interests... weren't entirely foolish. If Benyon could find a suitable mate, it gave them all hope.

"Ithann," Jaron said, approaching the man's back.

He knew the warrior heard him—Jaron saw his shoulders twitch slightly before he turned.

"Pacifist," Ithann said.

"It's Doctor. Your translator is faulty."

Ithann bared his teeth in a smile. "I'll have it maintenanced."

"I'm currently overseeing the trainee Mila's medical treatment. It's my recommendation she be placed on light duty for the foreseeable future."

"No."

Jaron paused. "No?"

Ithann crossed his arms. "She's lazy and clumsy- she'll either fall in or fall out."

Jaron stared at the man, not bothering to hide his scorn. "Are you a fool? She's ill, and pushing through with the training to the best of her ability. The exercise- to an extent- is beneficial to her. But I don't want her sparring."

The Adekhan turned away. "Then make her a medic. But while she trains with the warriors, she'll be expected to perform like a warrior. Or suffer the consequences."

"I don't think-"

Ithann whirled, stepping into Jaron's space, their chests bumping. Jaron shut his mouth, eyes narrowing.

"You were saying, *doctor*?"

Jaron counted one breath, the next, then stepped back. "I won't ask you again."

As he turned, Ithann grunted. "I know you won't."

Jaron knew Ithann didn't understand that he'd given a warning, not made a request.

He returned to his office, giving Stacia instructions that he wasn't to be disturbed for a thirty-minute reflection break. Entering the small room set aside for his use to complete paperwork and speak to patients outside of a medical setting, he closed the door behind him. Coolly surveyed the available wall space. And slammed his fist through a patch of smooth drywall. He examined the indentation with satisfaction and made a mental note to ask Stacia to arrange the repairs.

Jaron cleaned and bandaged his hand- for the benefit of the humans- and continued with the working day. He would see her that evening.

* * *

He'd vowed the path of non-violence. Since the use of brute force in resolving difficulties usually indicated a lack of sophisticated thinking, the vow was working for him. His parents would be pleased. Jaron himself would be more pleased, at this time, if his own intellect hadn't already calculated the outcome of forcing Mila into a relationship she didn't want.

This was one of those times he was seriously weighing the use of brute strength.

The sheer stupidity of enrolling in a medical trial floored him- he'd thought her more intelligent. But evidently when sick, human faculties dribbled out of their ears.

Money, she'd said. *Dying.* As if he would allow her to die. Jaron gritted his teeth, tattoos surging around his arms in reaction to his emotional disturbance. He wanted the woman- already considered her his, had staked a clear claim- and his body was tired of waiting. Fortunately for her, he wasn't ruled by his cock, or the urge to bond.

At least not yet.

He knocked on the door of her efficiency apartment. Jaron understood the reasoning behind human government housing single adults in bland, cramped buildings to conserve space, but that didn't mean their reasoning was ethical, or even healthy. The place stank, the construction clearly shoddy.

And what security was present at the front doors was disinterested at best.

She opened the door, circles under her eyes, a thin shirt hanging on her slumped frame. He wondered how much energy it had taken for her to get out of bed and open the door.

"Ah, shit, Jaron, I'm not in the mood," Mila said.

He slipped past her and closed the door. She sighed, saying nothing, and he led her to the donated couch in her tiny living room. When she settled next to him, he tugged the hem of her shirt, pulling it over her head. She wore another thin garment underneath and loose shorts.

"We can't keep doing this," she said.

Jaron didn't reply, pulling her onto his lap after discarding his shirt. She settled against his chest with a sigh as he wrapped one arm around her back and clasped her other at the wrist.

The tattoos swirled. Jaron grit his teeth as they divided, swarming over his arm and onto hers. Brightening, sending a flash of color and energy underneath her skin. Her full lips parted, lashes fluttering. Her hips arched into him, just a bit, but this time he didn't bother to dampen his reaction. His body hardened underneath her and she stiffened. He held her fast, staring into her face.

Let her understand exactly why he wouldn't allow her to die. Let her understand she had no choice but to live.

She wiggled as her energy returned, attempting to pull away. He snorted. As if.

"Be still," he said. "We need to have a frank discussion."

She stopped struggling, holding herself still. Jaron didn't know why Mila bothered to hide her desire from him- from herself. She refused to meet his eyes, pulse fluttering in her neck from the rapid pace of her heart. A faint flush under golden brown skin as her lips subtly plumped with blood.

His eyes lowered to her chest, laughably concealed by thin cloth. A small smile curved his lips as he watched her nipples pebble. One day soon he would take one in his mouth and suckle, play with her while his fingers plunged in and out of her pussy until she was slick and ready for him.

"I don't want to talk about it," she said.

At least she wouldn't pretend to misunderstand. "I never told you why I left the warrior's path for medicine."

Her head turned, eyes slowly rising to meet his. Reluctantly curious. Jaron didn't speak much about himself, or his life.

"My parents were doctors. Researchers. They studied plants and exotic disease."

Her eyes gleamed with flecks of gold swimming in green, bright from the strength he'd transferred to her.

"What happened?" she asked, voice soft.

Her perception pleased him. "We were on an exploratory mission on a strange planet, and they contracted an unknown disease. Something harmless to the natives, but deadly to us. They died."

She gasped, reaching up to cup his cheek. "I'm so sorry."

"It was a long time ago." But he didn't remove her hand. "I vowed, Mila, that I would never watch another person I cared about die from illness." Jaron caught her hand as she moved it, eyes lowering again. "I don't intend to break that vow with you."

"I- Jaron." She stopped, sighed. "There isn't anything anyone can do for me."

"What do you think we've been doing the last several months? Exploring alien-human diplomacy?"

Her expression tightened. "Delaying the inevitable. I don't even know why you like me."

His brow rose. "Why do you like me?"

Her watched the expressions cross her face. "You... we have good conversations. You understand me. You treat me like Mila, not like your sick cancer patient."

"I see you," he said, voice soft. "I see who you are now, and who you have the potential to be. You cared for your mother, even as a child, when she should have cared for you. Do you know how rare that strength is? That level of selflessness?"

It was what, inevitably, had drawn him to her. Or at least was beginning of what had drawn him to her. No child should have endured what she had endured. But she had, and survived, proving herself to be both warrior and healer, even if she didn't see herself that way.

He did. He was older- he knew better than her. He knew how to weigh a person and measure their worth.

She gazed at him. "And that's enough?"

Jaron knew what she was asking. "The ease we have with each other- that's rare as well, Mila." He lowered his head, lips brushing her ear- he wanted to be certain she heard him. Clearly. "You will not die. I won't allow it. I also won't allow you to fight me. Do you understand? I will save you- even against your will."

She shoved at his chest and this time he let her go. "You don't understand!"

Jaron rose, watching as she walked in hectic circles around the couch, rubbing her arms. The tattoos began to fade, dissolving as she instinctively rejected the bond. But they'd lasted a few minutes longer this time. He was patient. A few minutes longer each time was enough. One day she would accept him completely.

"Then explain. You're wasting your strength with all the pacing."

She whirled, glaring at him. "It's not about me. My mother-" she paused.

Jaron's brow rose. "Where *is* Ayita?"

"Back in the hospital." Mila grimaced. "She tried to overdose again."

"If you signed her over to my care-"

Mila shook her head. "No. I won't cage her, even to save her." Her lips pursed. "She's been taken advantage of enough."

Jaron tamped down his impatience. He knew the story- and he also knew it was an excuse. Ayita was destroying her daughter- and Mila was allowing it. Foolish humans.

"You were explaining why you think I shouldn't save your life."

She sighed. "It's just- I'm going to die anyway, no matter how long you prolong the inevitable. And... the treatment is so expensive. That's why I decided it would be better- I mean. The government has this program for Low Tier patients. If you forgo the treatment, they'll pay your surviving family a lifetime annuity. It's supposed to be cheaper than treating what I have."

Jaron had been with her for six months, courting her in his way, and not once had she told him this. He'd respected her privacy as she'd asked, though the request had been ridiculous and his compliance, for a doctor, even more so.

Anger surged. At her, at the human government. At his own patience for allowing her to keep things from him.

"This is about your guilt- the crutch you lean on to keep from being responsible for your life."

She took a step back, flinching from the whip of his tone. "That's not fair. My mother-"

"Is an adult. You aren't to blame for what happened to your mother. You aren't responsible for her."

Her fists balled at her sides. "Of course I'm responsible for her, you insensitive iceberg!"

He shook his head. "I should have pried this out of you months ago."

"Get out!"

Jaron snorted. "Make me."

Her mouth gaped a little. He smiled nastily- she wasn't used to him disobeying her. He'd practiced a careful, inoffensive aura, all the better to woo her with. Underneath the fatigue and foolish emotionalism was a woman with a delightful temper and intriguing will. He had to tread carefully or else she would fully reject him- and that he would not tolerate. She was his to save, his to heal. And when she was fully back to herself, he planned to reap all the benefits of his labor.

Forever.

3

"What's wrong with you?" Mila asked.

She'd known better than to admit the truth to him. Known he'd take her illness personally. Over the months of their friendship, he'd let more slip about his past than he probably thought. Mila had figured there was *something* somewhere that drove him. A Yadeshi warrior studying Earth medicine while he moonlighted as basically a sports clinic doc?

"How's your residency going?" she asked, distracted by her thoughts.

He shouldn't even be here right now- he should be at his research hospital. Not the same hospital hosting her clinical trial- she wasn't stupid- but another prominent institute in the city.

Jaron took a step forward. "Don't try and change the subject."

"Fine." She moved, sitting on the couch to disguise her retreat. Her body always felt better after the glowy alien thing- if better meant aggravatingly horny as well as ravenous for food. "Look, I'm dying- it's been going on a while. I probably should have told you before we started hanging out. It's not fair I guess." Who wanted to be friends with someone who was going to be literally gone in a few short years? "But you don't have to act all growly about it."

"How should I act, Mila? You've kept this from me and I could have solved this problem months ago."

"I don't think so. Look, Jaron, I'm tired-"

"Lie. I can hear your heartbeat. And scent your desire."

She blushed, his soft, knowing tone angering her. "So what? I can't control physiological reactions. Humans aren't like that. Why don't you just go? I need to rest and think."

Jaron took a liquid step forward, eyes narrow. "No."

"Please."

He paused, stared at her for a long minute, then looked away with a grimace. "Damn you. One day you'll be begging me to stay, Mila. Soon."

Mila locked the door behind him as he left, breathing unsteady. She'd seen the look in his eyes, known he was one wrong word- on her part- from... doing something. Something that would change everything, and she wasn't ready yet. This more aggressive side of him was less comfortable to handle. She'd thought he was going to argue with her all night, maybe insist on doing more of the glowy healy thingy.

Her cell rang. She didn't have one of the communication screens- her landlord was cheap. Well, her landlord was the government, and they defined all new levels of cheap. She hauled herself off the couch with a sigh, touching Accept.

"Mila," Dr. Strahler said. "How are you feeling today?"

The question wasn't perfunctory. Part of the clinical trial included a weekly check in call between face-to-face appointments.

"I feel fine, Dr.," Mila said. "Today's been good." Or at least the second half of the day, after Jaron's infusion of energy.

Rebecca's- the doctor insisted on being called by her first name, probably an attempt at a warm bedside manner- eyes flickered.

"You feel fine, Mila?"

Mila frowned, wondering why that was a problem. "Yeah. The morning started out a little iffy, but-"

"What time did you take your injection?"

"Around lunchtime, when the Adekhan let us have a break."

"And you didn't feel any of the usual side effects?"

Like dragging weariness, a mushy feeling in her mouth like her tongue was the consistency of applesauce. She *had* been feeling like that, but lately just being around Jaron seemed to counteract whatever problems the medication caused. Mila knew she couldn't say anything about that, though, and felt a little guilty.

"Not... really."

Because Jaron's treatment was interfering with the doctors, Mila knew whatever data they gleaned from her as a test subject would be flawed. But, damnit. What other choice was there? She needed the extra money, was squirreling away any spare half credit she could. When she died, her mother would be alone- but at least she would be able to pay for basic food, clothing and shelter for the rest of her life.

Ayita was still young. Maybe one day her mind would heal and she could have a real family. Mila would never have a real family- but maybe her mother could.

"Alright. That could be a good sign, or a sign the medication is no longer working. I'd like you to come in for your appointment a few days early."

Rebecca gave her a new date and time and signed off. Mila knew she'd have to be careful of what she said. Not just to avoid being kicked out of the program, but to avoid letting humans know that the Yadeshi were walking alien shamans.

The cell rang again just as she set it down, Mila snatched it back up as soon as she saw the caller ID.

"Yes?" Her fingers clenched the phone.

"Ms. Washington?"

"Yes, this is Mila Washington."

"Ma'am, we're calling to inform you that Ayita Washington checked herself out of the facility against doctor's advisement two hours ago."

Two hours... "You let her get a two-hour head start?"

"We apologize for the inconvenience; all documents have been properly signed. Have a nice evening."

The called disconnected and Mila whirled, pausing long enough to grab her t-shirt and gym shoes. Jaron couldn't be that far away.

She dialed his number, hoping he'd walked instead of driving the short distance from YETI to where she stayed.

"Mila?"

The sleek lines of his azure face filled the screen. "Jaron, I need your help."

"I'm turning around."

She waited in the parking lot, shifting from one foot to the other. Mila wanted to leave *now*, but knew where her mother had gone... it wouldn't be smart to not have backup in the form of some kind of person scarier than her. Jaron was *much* scarier than shesemi.

"Mila, what's wrong?"

She jumped, turning. Hadn't heard him creep up. "I hate when you walk so quiet."

His brow rose. "Mila."

"Mom checked herself out again."

He frowned. "Will she have gone to the same place as before?"

"The yellow house. Yes. Can you come with me? I don't want to go alone."

"Of course." But he didn't move, staring at her.

She couldn't read the expression in his cool eyes, other than to be sure he was trying to figure out all the angles. That was the problem with scientists. They never stopped thinking.

"Ok, what is it?" she asked.

"You know I think your mother would be better off at YETI."

"She's better off where *she* says she's better off. She has the right to make that choice, don't you think?"

"The right to choose ends when her life destroys yours."

It was a semi-old argument between them. "We can talk about it later. I don't want her in that house."

He reached out, taking her hand. Lifted her palm face up, studying the lines as if he could read her future. "I'll help you- but this time there's a price."

Her skin tingled, despite sudden apprehension. "A... price? Jaron, you know I don't have any money."

He shook his head slowly, eyes glinting. "You're deflecting. You know it's not money I want."

She opened her mouth, closed it. Damnit- if he'd been any other man, with the events of the day and his oddly intense behavior, she'd think... something she refused to think. Because even if there was hope for something *more*- she would be dead in a year. Two, tops.

"What do you want?" she asked, dreading the answer. Dreading having to tell a lie in order to get his help.

"A date."

Mila blinked. "Well, that's weird. What in the world would you do with dried fruit?"

His eyes narrowed. "Mila."

Well, she'd had to try. Abandoning the pretense of misunderstanding, she tugged her hand. His fingers slid up her wrist, holding her fast.

"I'm not letting you go until you give me the answer I want."

She scowled. "There's a name for men who behave like this."

Jaron laughed. "I don't care about names. I care about results."

"Fine, Jaron. You can have a date. I don't know what you think we're going to *do* with a date-"

"The usual things humans do." He smiled, teeth sharp, voice a low, deepening croon. A promise. An *uncivilized* promise.

"Alright, let me go," she said, tugging again, heart jumping. "You have drug dealers to beat up."

He released her hand. "Oh, I don't think it will come to that."

* * *

The owner of the house was waiting for Mila- not for Jaron, of course. No one expected her to show up with a tall, blue Clark Kent in tow.

"Where is she?" Mila asked, shoving the front door open.

The lanky young woman who'd opened it a crack stumbled back, swearing. It was a bad sign Mila didn't cough from the thick smoke- she'd become used to it over the years. If it was just a bunch of people chilling after work or otherwise minding their own business, she wouldn't care. But Samson preyed on the most vulnerable people in the city- people with chronic pain or mental issues.

"Sam!"

She searched the downstairs rooms. There was a living area with vintage bean bag cushions and a flat screen- news, of all things. The dining room table was cluttered with paraphernalia, bowls and chips and players huddled around cards. Not seeing Ayita, she took the stairs to the second level two at a time. The people mostly ignored her- no one here cared about anything but their own business.

"Wonderful place," Jaron said behind her. "The decor is especially stimulating."

A Yadeshi joking about feng shui. Now her day was complete. Mila walked down a long hallway to a bedroom with its door half cracked. More noise from a television set, lights on low. Her mother curled up on a bed, asleep, Samson stretched beside her, vapor flowing from his lips as a remote dangled from his fingers. She'd never seen him in anything but a plain t-shirt and jeans, hair cut in a low buzz.

He glanced over as Mila entered, eyes widening a bit when Jaron stepped into sight. "Hey, Mila. Thought you'd be by. Gave her a shower and a joint. Wouldn't eat but you can take a sandwich with you."

Mila inhaled, exhaled. "You know she can't be here at all. You were supposed to not let her in if she came back."

"What, you want me to kick her on the street when she's out of it? Grow up, girl. Ain't nothin' going on here that's gonna make your mama any sicker than she already is."

Mila approached the bed, crouching down to study her mother's face. Thin, brown skin pale from several weeks being indoors. Her long curls were damp, and ruthlessly contained in two tight braids. When she was sleeping Mila remembered just how young Ma was. But then, it wasn't like she ever really forgot.

"I just wish..." she trailed off, not bothering.

"No point," Sam said. "Till she decides to help herself, ain't nothin' you can do. So what's with the bodyguard?" Sam jerked his head at Jaron. "No one here gonna bother you, girl."

"Yeah, I figured since she owes you money you'd cop a 'tude about me taking her."

She glanced at him sideways and pressed on him the desire to just let them walk out peacefully- he could deal with Ayita and her tab later.

Sam smiled, and it wasn't pleasant. "I bide my time, girl. One day- but for now, get out."

* * *

Mila didn't know how long her mind trick would work.

"You can't keep doing that," Jaron said.

"What?"

He glanced at her. "Don't pretend with me, Mila. I know what you're doing. The... healings... are increasing certain latent abilities in you. I can feel it. It doesn't always happen with humans, but when it does, they need to be trained."

Her mouth tightened. "If you knew it was a possibility, why didn't you say something? I thought I was going crazy for a while." But she'd always had a strong will, especially before she became sick.

"Usually it happens with humans who have a predilection towards telepathy."

She nodded. Several times in her life she'd been able to influence others. Nothing major, and not in ways that would make any dramatic changes in her life, but just enough to smooth a bad situation into a tolerable one.

"We'll talk about it later. Let's just get clear of this block before Sam tries something."

Jaron carried Ayita who was so deeply asleep Mila knew Sam had given her more than a joint. Probably pills, too, so he didn't have to deal with her frenetic energy. He and Ayita went way back- Mila didn't want to think about what kind of way back, though. Her mother didn't have to do those things anymore; she'd managed to get well enough with treatment.

Looking over her shoulder, she walked faster. There were enough working street lights that Jaron's face shone a weird orange blue, but in some areas of the neighborhood where the lights didn't reach, there were black spots. Patches where an attacker could wait, scope out prey.

"Not much longer," Jaron murmured, catching Mila's eyes as she looked back again.

"I don't like it," she said. "Last time I saw Samson he was pissed about me not being able to pay Ma's tab."

"Walk faster."

It took her a moment to realize the calm command wasn't simply a response to her words. A figure stepped out of a black spot, a bit of alley behind an abandoned corner store. She only saw the shadow because Jaron was watching it.

"Shit," she said.

"Your right," he said.

She looked in that direction, picked out two more shadows, emerging from either side of the street. Jaron stopped, set Ayita on the sidewalk, propped against a building.

"They might not be for us," she said.

He threw her a disbelieving look. "Guard your mother."

"You're a doctor!"

But he ignored her hissed words and Mila swore in frustration. What the hell was he going to do against three attackers?

There was no foreplay, no preliminaries like in the movies. One moment Jaron was within speaking distance, and the next the three converged on him.

4

Mila didn't scream, that would just be stupid and remind one of the three that she was a sitting duck. But damn- he wasn't a warrior. He might have trained as a teenager, but he was a medic. They were lucky this was a mostly abandoned section of retail shops, rather than residential. There would be almost no traffic at night and few residents to potentially involve law enforcement. The next block with houses was still almost three streets down.

Jaron leapt away from a blow, sweeping into an advanced Form- one she'd seen the fourth year trainees practicing. How much longer could he hold out against three humans versed in dirty street fighting?

"Hold tight, Ma," she said under her breath and strode forward.

No illusions about how much help she could be- half trained and physically weak. But she supposed she could at least act as a minor annoyance and distraction so Jaron could fight better. She couldn't do the mind thingy and fight at the same time- she'd tried that once before and it hadn't ended well. Jaron barely seemed to be moving, his Forms perfect, but... lazy. Almost rote, without the fire of the Adekhans in battle.

She sighed and flowed into Sixth Form, the first of the offensive skills taught once the basic defensive Forms were mastered. Not that she'd mastered them- Ithann loved to reiterate how hopelessly clumsy she was- but at least she had a little extra oomph tonight and might not trip over her own feet.

"What are you doing!" Jaron roared, more an expression of outrage than an actual question.

A fist to her face she blocked just in time, spinning and aiming her foot in a snap kick.

"Helping!" she screamed back, a little offended at his tone.

"I told you to stay with Ayita!"

"Stop yelling at me and fight!"

She couldn't really pay attention to what he was doing, beleaguered as she was by her own opponent- who was playing with her more than anything else, if the huge, taunting grin was any indication. But Mila got the sudden impression of speed, and air. Oomphs and cut off cries and then the shuffling of shoes on pavement decreased by at least one as a body went flying through the air.

"Fuck," she said, but the body wasn't blue.

The moment of inattention cost her. Her opponent stopped smiling and attacked in earnest. The sophistication and oddness of her fighting style kept her from getting her ass kicked immediately. She managed to parry blows and only take a few glancing hits, but anger rose as she found herself stressed, unable to return blow for blow. Her breath came harsher, Jaron's healing draining rapidly.

Rage in the back of her mind, masculine rage. Her knees buckled, Mila gritting her teeth to remain upright, when her body seized.

* * *

Jaron stopped playing with them the moment he felt Mila at his back. Damn foolish female. The young warriors always wanted to leap into battle before they were ready.

He disabled and tossed the humans away from him just as Mila's body jerked, sending her sprawling to the ground.

"*Fuck.*"

The human she'd been fighting turned and sprinted away as Jaron lunged forward. He didn't give the assailant another thought, grabbing Mila's head between his hands and straddling her flailing body. He pushed a shockwave of energy into her, a pulse that loosened her muscles and sent her into unconsciousness. She hadn't bit her tongue. Jaron calculated his options, realizing he now had two women to deal with. A quick glance showed Ayita was still where he'd left her, and unharmed.

But Mila jerked again. Jaron stared for a split second, then scowled. Damnit, even asleep she was rejecting his healing. He lifted her in his arms, pulling her shirt up enough for him to slide skin against skin and opened the bond between them.

Jaron sucked in a breath, hissing. The darkness swirling inside her. A cesspit of guilt and anguish, pain over years of neglect and loneliness. A desperate need for security and… family. Home. But, the guilt. Ayita must have been a beautiful girl, before Mila. Must have been happy and promising, before Mila. Mila's fault, the unwanted baby, the product of assault. Daily reminder of pain, Ayita's constant walking bruise.

He pulled out of the surface layers of her mind, cursing his own forcefulness in trying to heal her. He'd breached her natural mental barriers, felt things he had no right to know. But the feelings confirmed what he already knew; Mila felt guilty for her conception. Felt guilty for Ayita's shell of a life.

If he wanted her to accept the bond, fight to live, he had to convince her that her life was worth living.

Glancing at Ayita, his eyes narrowed. He'd have to convince Ayita to live as well.

* * *

Jaron decided to take the women back to YETI rather than to a hospital. Ayita needed rest and Mila needed what he could provide- human medicine wouldn't do anything for her in the long term. He called and arranged for a vehicle to transport them, remaining on alert for more attackers.

He put off explanations when they arrived at the complex, having Ayita lodged in a small singlet room and taking Mila to his suite. Because he was on a long term assignment, they given him a larger apartment than most of the Yadeshi on earth. And because he was a doctor and seen as less hardy than a warrior. Jaron snorted. He didn't care what anyone thought of him- if thinking he was delicate earned him larger accommodations, he was fine with the misconception.

Jaron monitored Mila's condition for a while longer, settling her on the bed and making sure she was comfortable. He kept a thin tendril of the unformed bond open between them, just enough to alert him to any strong emotions while he went to have a talk with Ayita.

Mila's mother was still asleep when he arrived, having detoured to his office for a syringe filled with a compound that would wake up a full grown *ghagreuth*. He was reasonably sure it would work on a human- they had equivalent creatures in their Earth elephants, so he imagined the concept was the same. Besides, he'd used it in smaller doses before to aid fatigued students needing an extra boost, with no ill side effects.

Jaron injected Ayita and waited, calculating the odds that the substance would interact with anything she may have taken. Ayita began coughing, eyelids fluttering, and woke up with a startled snort.

"Ah, fuck, where am I?"

She sat up, Jaron leaning back to avoid her forehead smashing into his.

"Ayita."

She glanced at him, tired dark eyes wide. "Jar Jar! What's going on? Where's Sam?"

"Mila and I retrieved you. Mila is unwell."

She glanced around, probably taking in her surroundings. Not many human dwellings appropriated Yadeshi decor. And she wasn't stupid.

"We're at YETI? Where's Mila?"

"Asleep." He paused. "She seized."

Ayita grimaced, shoulders slumping. "Ah, my baby. I thought she was getting better."

"That's what we need to talk about." He set aside the syringe and rose, affixing a pleasant expression on his face as she eyed him warily. "There are some papers I want you to sign. We'll talk about what is in it for you."

* * *

Mila awoke, head pounding and mouth dry. It wasn't like in books where she had to remember where she was or anything melodramatic- she already knew. The place smelled like him, and the decor certainly wasn't anything human inspired.

Sitting up, her head didn't swim. Her thinking felt clear, vision sharp. Was this what it felt like to be healthy?

On top of that feeling came resigned anger.

Jaron.

He entered as she was swinging off the bed to her feet, stopping just inside the bedroom door. He watched her, expression anticipatory in a vulpine, nearly smug fashion.

"You did the glowy thing while I was out, didn't you?"

"You feel better."

"Much better. Good enough to knock you out."

He smiled, eyes gleaming. "I'm delighted you want to try. Ayita is having a meal. You should join her. I've sent the kitchen a diet plan for the both of you for the next several weeks. You have vitamin deficiencies I'd like corrected."

She stared at him. "You drew my blood?"

"I'm your attending physician. I have to have information to develop a proper treatment plan."

"You high handed blue bug."

He lifted a hand. "You'll appreciate the rationality of my actions once you've become used to operating at full strength."

Mila sighed, frustrated, and walked towards him. "That's the problem, though. It's temporary."

"It doesn't have to be," he said as she pushed past him.

She stopped in the middle of the living room, taking a deep breath. "It's not just about how long it lasts. It's about the possibility of it lasting. I don't want it to last, Jaron. I need to die."

"You want to atone for what happened to your mother."

Mila turned. "Do you understand that? Atonement?"

His eyes showed no emotion. "Of course. But atonement isn't yours to pay- it's your father's."

"He isn't here, he can't pay. I'm his daughter."

He didn't respond right away. "Normally, I would agree with you. But this circumstance is one of the few where a child should not be responsible for the crimes of the family."

"But there's a concept in Yadeshi culture- a family assuming responsibility to a victim?"

"Of course." He moved forward, closing the distance between them.

"But, Mila- your mother doesn't want your penance. She's in enough pain. How do you think she will feel, suffering the same crime twice? Did you think your death wouldn't harm her?"

"Of course it will! But she won't know it could have been prevented. And the government will take care of her."

"I will tell her."

His words robbed the breath from her lungs. It took her several tried to begin speaking. "You wouldn't."

Merciless eyes. Eyes as blue as deep night, as unyielding. "What do humans say? Try me."

Anger fled, the heat of the emotion robbing her bones of marrow. She collapsed against his chest, grief too great even for tears. He held her anyway, arms wrapping around her and holding her close as she wept silently. She should hate him. Somehow she couldn't.

"I spoke with Ayita," he said after a while, voice soft and deep. "She's signing herself into YETI. She'll be under my guardianship."

Mila didn't move for a moment. "Are you sure?"

"Mila."

Her head rose. He searched her face and then his lips curved. "Good. You'll become used to the idea of living soon. I plan to give you a very good reason."

She sniffed, not pretending to misunderstand. "Sex? That doesn't really mean anything."

His brow rose. "Is that a challenge?"

Mila scowled. "No. That's stupid."

"But still a challenge."

She wasn't surprised when he lowered his head, lips brushing against hers with the comfortable warmth of familiarity- except they'd never kissed before. But he felt old, familiar. Undemanding.

Mila softened against him, sliding an arm around his back. Muscles flexed under her touch, his body shifting slightly. She tensed, but he didn't move. His tongue traced her bottom lip, teeth nipping gently. A gentle tingle tickled her core, her body encouraging further exploration.

He pulled away, eyes studying her, a sheen of warmth peeking through the impassiveness. "Good?"

"I… yes." She was good. She stared up at him, surprised and pleased.

"Again?"

She licked her lips. "Okay."

"Somewhere more comfortable, I think."

She squeaked involuntarily when he lifted her into his arms. Once, a long time ago, she'd been a pleasingly plump girl. Her illness and effects of the treatment had slowly leached away her figure. Maybe now that she was getting better- thanks to Jaron, damnit- she could start putting on weight again.

He took her into his sleeping area, laying her down on the bed and stretching out next to her, propping his head on an elbow as he studied her. Mila stared back at him, a little annoyed.

A smile curved his lips. "I've heard human women must say 'yes' at each stage of a seduction."

"So you're waiting for me to wave a big white flag of surrender?"

He laughed, covering her with his body. "I think I'd like that, Mila. I should take advantage now while you're not yet at full strength."

His thumb brushed her lips, fingers trailing down her skin. He cupped her breast and she hissed from the sudden contact, back arching.

"Yes?" he murmured.

He lowered his head, mouth replacing his hands. Even through her t-shirt, the touch seared her skin. The muscles of her inner thighs relaxed, preparing to spread wide for his pleasure; for hers.

"What are we doing?" she gasped.

His mouth moved to her neck, teeth nipping her skin, biting down, not quite gently.

"Exploring."

Another bite, lips on hers, hot and demanding as he released a little more of his strength, relaxed a bit more into her body. He was holding back; she was beginning to realize that. Could her laid back, snarky, blue Clark Kent have a darker side?

Of course he did. He was a Yadeshi warrior, even if he now practiced healing. She'd be stupid to think his gentleness with her was a lack of strength, or intensity.

"I can feel your panic, Mila," Jaron said, lips on her jaw. "You're safe with me."

"I know, I- what are we doing?"

He sighed, pulled back. "Let's take it a day at a time and find out. But for now we need to go speak with Ayita."

Some of the pleasant glow evaporated in the face of reality. "I know."

Jaron rose from the bed and took her hand, pulling her to her feet. As she walked past him she thought she saw a flicker in his eyes, a slight narrowing as a decidedly ungentle smile curved his mouth. But when she paused and looked over her shoulder, he was following at her heels with his usual bland expression.

Must have been the light.

5

Unexpectedly, he left Mila to talk to Ayita alone.

"Resolve your issues," he said, though his face wasn't unkind.

"Not that simple," she muttered, knocking on her mother's door.

Ayita opened it a moment later, glancing down the hall as Jaron turned a corner.

"Hi, Ma."

Ayita stepped back so Mila could enter. She stopped in the middle of the room- one single unit efficiency was just like another- then turned. Ayita stood at the door, hands at her sides.

"Jaron says you're going to get better," her mother said.

"Yeah. Looks like."

Ayita blinked rapidly. "Good. I'm okay with being here, Mimi. It's a decent place."

She studied her mother. "You know you don't have to do this for me. The whole program, being under Jaron's patronage. He's a bossy bug."

Her mother smiled a little. "I think it will be okay. It's time we both started to live."

Mila took a deep breath. She wanted to believe her mother so badly. "What makes this time different?"

How many times had Ayita promised a change? That she would get help for her pain, stop the drugs and be a mother to Mila? How many times had Mila checked herself into a children's home so she could get a few days of regular meals and peace from her mother before running away home- because she knew Ayita couldn't take care of herself?

Ayita's eyes were dark, her brow tight. "I think I'm just ready now. To heal. It's why I left the hospital. I realized it wasn't where I needed to be."

"And went to *Samson's*."

Ayita sniffed. "I have unfinished business with him, don't worry about that." Her mother paused for a moment, voice quieting. "I don't want to lose you because I was weak."

"You're not *weak*, mother," Mila whispered, hands clenching. "No one helped you, not even your own mother."

Ayita smiled, a sad quirk of her lips. "And I didn't help you. But you're going to break that cycle. Your children will have the mother they deserve."

Her mother came forward, touched Mila's cheek. "Let's start over, okay? And it looks like you could use something to eat."

* * *

She stayed long enough to eat a meal with her mother and then left for her assigned room. The reflective, quiet, striving for calm Ayita was someone new- Mila wasn't sure how to handle her now that her mother seemed to want to reverse their roles back to where they should have always been. Ayita Mom, Mila Child.

But Mila agreed to stay in the complex while her mother adjusted. Gayle dropped by her new quarters, prowling the small student efficiency with the restless energy and long legs of a panther.

"You're going to stick with the training, right?" Gayle asked, and finally choose a portion of the floor to stretch out on.

"Yes. I'm getting stronger."

Gayle's eyes were sharp, knowing. "I think I know why, too."

Mila hadn't told her, mostly because Gayle had a big mouth, no shame, and a propensity to meddle.

"I'm going to take *everything* slow."

"We can do some extra sessions, maybe get you caught up on the forms if you're feeling better." Gayle stretched, rolling onto her back. "I'll talk to Ithann, too. He really is an ass, but if you know how to work around him, he can be handled."

Mila arched a brow. "You're going to *handle* an Adekhan?"

Gayle's smile was all predator. "It gives me something extra to do."

WARRIOR'S VOW
***

Mila returned to her apartment outside YETI to gather Ayita's clothing and personal items. Plus, she had her appointment at the medical center. Jaron might not like it, but she would continue to participate until she could figure out a plan for the future. When her health was completely improved, she would need to begin applying for work again- and it had been two years since she'd been granted medical disability. In order to become marketable, she might have to enroll in a government funded training program, gain some new skills.

Fun.

Mila took a duffel bag of her mother's things with her to the appointment, not wanting to double back afterward. The building was a glass and metal structure, the lobby open all the way to the top of the building, letting in light. Everything sleek, high tech and expensive looking.

She took the elevator to the seventh floor, entering a quiet, blue carpeted hallway with glass for walls allowing a view of the lobby below. Entering the office, she signed in, sat down, and waited. But not long.

Dr. Strahler emerged from the white door leading to the medical areas. "Mila? Come with me, I'm ready for you."

Good, that meant it would be a brief appointment and she could get back to YETI before Jaron started asking questions.

Rebecca walked briskly, Mila pleased that she was able to keep up with the doctor.

"You look well, Mila. I was curious about how you seem to be responding to the treatment."

Mila said nothing. She'd spent the bus ride trying to figure out what to say without actually lying. Being a terrible liar. Because historically she had no energy to tell lies. Rebecca held the door to the small bay open and Mila walked in, setting her things down and hopping up on the bench.

"We'll want to do some blood work, of course. And maybe a series of endurance tests."

Mila's heart sank a bit. So it would be a more comprehensive exam. No choice though, if she wanted to continue receiving the stipend.

"No problem," she responded because the doctor appeared to be waiting for a reply.

The blood work and tests took over an hour and the doctor left her in the room for twenty minutes. Mila took the time to attempt to nap, but wound up pacing the small area instead.

The door opened. "Mila, have a seat."

The tone put her on alert. "Is something wrong?"

Rebecca smiled, the expression too… bright. "Not at all! In fact, I have excellent news. Your preliminary results show such promise that we've decided it would be well to have you check into the facility for more in depth examination. This comes with a substantial bonus, of course."

Greed notwithstanding, Mila wasn't stupid. "No, I don't think I'd like that. I'll stick with just the basic care and stipend. I have responsibilities I can't really get out of."

Rebecca took a seat, smile fading. "Mila, we really need to know what's going on with your body. There are some odd things happening that necessitate future research. Whatever responsibilities you have, I can have the staff assist you with making arrangements."

Mila rose from her seat. "No, I'm sorry. Can you just sign off on the paperwork so I can go? I'll schedule the next appointment at the regular interval."

Dr. Strahler also rose. "Mila-"

"I said no!"

She strode out of the office and down the hall, Rebecca hard on her heels.

"Mila! Mila, stop. It's fine if you don't want to check in."

Mila slowed down, stopped.

"Can I ask you to schedule your next appointment for a week from now rather than the standard interval?"

She nodded, though reluctant. She couldn't afford to be too uncooperative. She'd have to talk to Jaron- he would be upset she'd ignored his request to withdraw from the program.

"That's fine," she said.

"Good. The nurse will have your medication ready."

WARRIOR'S VOW
* * *

But she remained tense over the next two days. Rebecca hadn't liked her refusal, had simply tried to put Mila at ease. Likely so she wouldn't withdraw from the program. Mila still needed to speak to Jaron about what the research might be able to find from her blood work, but found herself hesitant to broach the subject.

"Mila, don't be stupid," Gayle told her. "You have to let him know what's going on, if only so he can treat you properly. Drug interactions are no joke."

She finally made the decision to talk to him when she received an email from SIA.

Communication from SIA was never good.

Skimming the email, her heart sank even as anger rose, choking her breath. Damn the doctor. She knew that somehow Rebecca was behind this notification.

It was before her training for the day started, so she veered towards Jaron's office, blood boiling. Having enough civility not to barge in on him while he was with a client, Mila jerked her head towards the office to let Stacia know where she was headed. She'd discovered a few months ago Jaron had left instructions she wasn't to be prevented from seeing him at any time. The preferential treatment both warmed her and came in handy.

She stewed in his office, swiping a piece of candy from the bowl on his desk, grimacing at the taste. The Yadeshi like their desserts savory, which wasn't necessarily a bad thing- but sugar never hurt anyone. If she were rich she'd make a fortune introducing them all to chocolate.

Jaron entered not long after. "Mila, what's wrong?"

She was sprawled on the low couch set against one wall, an arm over her eyes.

"Who said anything is wrong?"

"I can feel it. Which you would know if you bothered to lower your barriers a bit."

What she lowered was her arm, to glare at him. "I don't know if I like the side effects of this glowy thingy. I don't want you reading my emotions."

WARRIOR'S VOW

He stood over her, arms at his side. Patient. "It goes both ways. Stop whining. What's wrong?"

"That bitch at the research place wanted me to check in so they could study some weird properties in my blood work. Would you happen to know anything about that?"

His expression shifted, a thinning of the lips and tightening around his eyes. "I asked you not to return there. And now you understand why."

"It used to be a free country. I said no, but she forwarded my test results to the state." Tears pricked her eyes. Anger, frustration, the desire to shred something. She rose to her feet, pacing. "They kicked me out of the survivor's program."

The enormity of it punched her in the gut. She needed those monthly payments- didn't want to go into a work gang while applying for skills programs. For a second she struggled to breathe.

Warm hands on her shoulders. "Mila, take a deep breath. Calm down."

She turned in his arms, balled up her fist and socked him in the chest.

He blinked, then smiled. "You're feeling much better. That's good."

Mila opened her mouth to reply when her cell went off. She fished it out of her pocket, scowling when she saw the number.

Glancing at Jaron, she pushed Accept. "That was some dirty shit you did, Rebecca."

The doctor smiled. "Good afternoon, Mila. Even though you no longer qualify for the program, I still wanted to check up on you."

"You can go to hell."

"If you would consider re-enrolling in our short term stay program, I'm sure I could notify the State that you meet the requirements to continue the survivor's benefits stipend."

Mila held the screen up to her nose. "Read my lips. Do you see my lips? Good. *No.* I'm not letting you experiment with me. You aren't getting any more blood samples."

"If you have something to hide-"

"Yeah, my ass, in your face."

She disconnected the call and look at Jaron, whose eyes were slightly wider than before.

"Well," he said. "I know being ill suppresses one's true personality, but I wasn't quite expecting..." he trailed off as she glared at him.

"What?"

He shook his head. "Never mind, Mila. The next few months should be interesting. Do you feel up to our date tonight?"

Anger fled. "Uh... our date?" Mila cleared her throat, not liking the squeaky sounds emerging.

He stepped closer, matching her when she backed up towards the desk. He really was... tall.

"Remember? You made a promise. I'm collecting."

6

He picked her up.

She hadn't expected him to actually pick her up- her apartment wasn't far from YETI and they'd always walked everywhere or taken public transportation. She hadn't even known he had access to a vehicle.

Mila stared at the two seater standing transport in the latest model. Sleek, black all over with tinted windows. As she came close the door slid open, revealing her blue alien.

He should have looked odd, large tip-tilted eyes and tousled blue black hair. The Yadeshi bone structure she could only describe as elfish, like in human fairy tales. Maybe the Yadeshi were the elves. Or the Vulcans.

"Coming?" he asked. "I read I am supposed to emerge from the vehicle and open the door for you- but the door opens on its own, and the book was published nearly 100 years ago, so I was uncertain if it would be considered outdated advice."

It was the most words she'd ever heard him say in one sentence outside of his medical office. Was he nervous? Looking into his eyes as she stepped into the transport and leaned her back along the rest, she knew he wasn't nervous. Safety restraints snapped into place and they were off.

"It probably is," she said. "Besides, opening a door is stupid. It means you think I need help handling simple shit."

He glanced at her again, after putting the vehicle on auto pilot. "It's not a sign of deference? We make such gestures for our political elders."

"That's different." Was she really discussing modern day feminism with an alien?

"You look nice."

He brushed her cheek with a finger, eyes moving along her body. She blushed. She'd come back to the apartment because none of the clothing at YETI was dateish. Not that she owned anything dateish. But between black leggings, glittery flats she'd found at a thrift center years ago, and a black t-shirt edged in lace, she'd managed to clean up a bit. She'd brushed a bit of olive oil into her hair and used some of her meager store of cosmetics, purchased when she'd started looking so haggard at the beginning of her illness.

"Thanks. Where are we going?"

"Downtown. There's an outdoor concert and wine garden. A festival, I'm told."

Which meant all kinds of people from different Tiers, wearing different clothes and mingling. She brightened. She'd been afraid he'd take her somewhere nice and she'd look like the kitchen help in comparison. But outdoors at night, her black would blend in and no one would notice. Or care.

"Great," she said. "I haven't heard live music in a long time."

His eyes warmed. "Good."

* * *

They sat on a wide grassy lawn, Jaron having purchased a thin blanket from a street vendor near the concert. She'd enjoyed the music, and he'd let her just sit and relax rather than blab at her. But then, Jaron had never been much to talk simply for the sake of talking. They'd argued over politics, history, philosophy- Earth and Yadeshi- but he still never spoke unless there was a point.

She liked that about him. Who wanted a man who didn't know when to shut up? He surprised her during the concert with a meal, having arranged with a nearby Italian restaurant to send a server with a brown bag filled with containers of salad, pasta and even a lush chocolate dessert.

"It's amazing the Yadeshi can eat human food," she said, eyeing him as he packed away a pound of alfredo.

"It required some modifications," he said. "But I enjoy human food. For the most part. The things you make in your factories are a crime against the universe, however."

She couldn't disagree, especially since the pasta tasted handmade. It didn't have the processed, machine cut look of grocery store stuff.

After the concert they continued to sit, sipping wine and watching as people gradually left the area for the blocks where all the restaurants and clubs were waiting to absorb the traffic.

Mila watched people wander, laughing and nibbling bites of street food when a flash of blue caught her eye. Blue was guaranteed to catch any human's attention these days, though.

Mila blinked, squinting as the couple slowly came closer. They hadn't noticed her and Jaron yet- though plenty of people had their eyes both on Mila and her date, and now the new human-Yadeshi pair.

"Is that Gayle?" Jaron asked.

Well, she had to believe her eyes, but she didn't really want to. "And... Adekhan Ithann."

"Intriguing." Cool interest in Jaron's tone. "One hopes Gayle knows what she is doing."

Mila saw the minute her best friend notched them. A huge grin broke out on Gaye's face and she grabbed Ithann's hand, dragging him forward in her mad sprint.

"This should be fun," Jaron murmured.

Mila didn't quite agree.

"Mila! Great minds and all that. We could have done a double date."

Jaron coughed at the same moment Ithann said, "I think not."

The men exchanged stiff nods while Gayle threw herself into the grass next to Mila, eyeing the mostly empty plate of appetizers next to Mila.

"Avoli Osteria," Gayle said. "Dope."

Only a High Tier woman would recognize fancy food just from the crumbs. It amused Mila anyway. For some reason her and Gayle just clicked, despite their vastly different backgrounds. A poor girl in and out of foster homes as her mother struggled with mental illness. A rich girl with a private school education and trust fund. But she supposed their differences complemented each other.

Mila cleared her throat. "So... are you and Adekhan... talking?"

Gayle's grin was wicked, dark eyes glinting maliciously as Ithann stiffened, arms crossed on his chest.

"Honey, you know I don't let a man get away with just *talking*."

"I applaud your choice," Jaron said, addressing Ithann.

Mila glanced at Jaron, eyebrow raised. The undertone of the words indicated he meant something else.

"We will see," Ithann said. "Training is not yet complete."

"Ah. Good luck with training."

Ithann's pale eyes narrowed. "And how fares your endeavor? Has it yielded fruit?"

Gayle and Mila exchanged glances. Obviously the men thought she and Gayle wouldn't understand they were discussing their relationships. Gayle rolled her eyes and rose.

"I'll take mine away before he says something to get in the dog house. Hey- we should do dinner at Dad's this month."

Mila winced. "I'm not up to the décor in your dad's house."

Gayle waved a hand even as she began tugging Ithann away. "I'll take you shopping. I have nothing better to do with my money anyway."

"That's a damn shame, Gayle Oba-"

Jaron clapped a hand over her mouth, halting her shout. "Don't say that name aloud. Let her keep her privacy."

Mila nodded, chastened. She forgot, sometimes, the burden Gayle carried.

He removed his hand. "That will be an interesting bond if it works."

"I knew there was something there, but I thought she was really just playing with him."

"Ithann does not play. Neither do I."

Mila tensed.

"Are you enjoying our date?" he asked.

"Of course."

He picked up her hand, thumb caressing her skin. "You enjoy being with me. I can tell."

"Whoa, you gotta do something about that lack of self-confidence, Jaron."

Jaron smiled, vulpine. "Healthy long term relationships are based in mutual friendship, respect and compatibility. The research-"

Mila groaned. "Please."

"Very well. But there is one other vital component that we have yet to fully explore."

She licked her lips. "What is that?"

He released her hand. "I have something to show you."

Mila watched as he reached in his pocket. He withdrew a slim rectangular disc with a series of flat black buttons.

"What is that?" she asked.

"Observe."

He set it in the grass, pressing a button. The air wavered and then-

Mila shrieked. "What the hell! Where are we?"

She waved her hand in front of her face- at least having the presence of mind to wave the empty hand and not the one clutching her wine. Nothing. She wasn't there.

"It's an invisibility shield," Jaron's disembodied voice said. "The range is short- there is only enough power to cloak two people and only for about an hour." He paused, and sounded sheepish. "It's a discount model."

Discount model, her behind.

Mila took a deep breath, heart rate slowing down. So she was invisible? It was just a trick of technology.

"So, what's the reason we're sitting here all see through?"

Fingers skimmed her shoulder, ran down her arm, causing the fine hairs to stand to attention.

"What are you doing?"

As if she had to ask. Mila had the presence of mind, as fingers slid under her shirt, skimming up her ribs to cup her breasts, to wince at her own inanity.

Lips on her neck as a warm, hard body settled over her, gently pressing her into the ground. He was moving a little fast, skipping the whole kiss and then seek permission part of things. But her submission permeated the bond, along with his hunger. Their hunger.

"Better than VR," she muttered, gasping when he nipped her in response.

He tugged her shirt over her head, a silent, invisible presence. Like a genie, or a god. A phantom for her pleasure.

The early evening breeze nipped at her exposed skin. She shivered, though not from cold. His hair brushed against her sensitized nipples, hot breath on the swell of her flesh right before he unsnapped and pushed aside her flimsy bra and claimed a nipple.

Mila ran her fingers through his hair. Heavy strands with a slight texture; like rough silk.

A couple walked past them and Mila froze, seeing the edge of someone's shoe.

"That woman almost stepped on me," she whispered in a strangled voice.

He said nothing, but his hand traveled to the waistband of her leggings, and tugged.

"Jaron," she hissed.

His caresses stopped. "Will you deny me?"

Mila licked her lips. "What... do you want to do?"

He shifted, and she was suddenly dissatisfied with his clothed state and began fumbling for the buttons of his shirt. Jaron helped, his heat moving away, the rustle of cloth settling onto grass in a heap. And then he was over her again, this time the full furnace of his smooth skin and hard chest crushing hers.

"Everything," he said. "I want to do everything. But not yet. For now, just an appetizer."

He tugged at her leggings again and this time she lifted her hips, allowing him to pull down the cloth. She laid completely naked beneath him, fully exposed to the world.

"That thing won't lose its power charge will it?" she asked.

He laughed softly. "It will beep a five-minute warning. Don't worry, Mila. No man other than I will ever see you."

Lips claimed hers, Mila's legs wrapping around his waist, opening herself to him. He fondled her nub, rolling and flicking the stiffening flesh between two fingers as she arched her hips in response.

Mila kissed him with increasing desperation, tongues clashing, his hold on her tightening, the hard length of him pulsing against her. The only barrier his loose pants.

She could just reach down, pull his cock out, and slip it inside her. Jaron moved down her body, Mila's legs falling to the ground, spread wide.

He nipped and suckled, licked and caressed her flesh until her found what he wanted. Mouth replaced fingers and suddenly he was inside her; fingers plunging into her cavern as he teased her clit.

It was quick; her body starved. Mila screamed when her orgasm crested. He slapped a hand over her mouth, holding back her cries.

People passing by glanced around, but saw nothing. Mila watched them through a daze of pleasure. And a slight feeling of dissatisfaction, despite her body's satiation.

"I want more," she whispered. "Let me taste you."

"I'm too big for your mouth."

The words, the husky, dark tone and the image they produced, spurred her hunger.

"Why are we waiting? I want *more*."

He crawled up her body. She tasted herself on his lips when he kissed her, brief but fierce. "Endure the torment. I have."

"You... bastard."

Jaron laughed. "I'll enjoy making you wait."

7

Her body ached. When she looked at him now, her womb clenched and the cavern between her thighs moistened, craving him.

He continued to torment her. Every evening, playing with her breasts and her pussy. Making her scream with pleasure but not allowing her to touch him in return. At times she saw cruelty mingled with satisfaction in his eyes and realized he enjoyed her sensual suffering, payback for his months of waiting. Though he would call it balancing the scales.

What sweet torment.

Jaron allowed Ayita to watch from the observation area for the next several days, under his hovering gaze. Mila felt odd with her mother's eyes on her, and even odder still as Ayita's deteriorated health slowly came back to life. It seemed Jaron was taking care of both mother and daughter. He wouldn't discuss Ayita's care with Mila other than to say her mother was on a strict whole foods diet, potent supplements and exercise in reasonable intervals as her body developed endurance. Years of abuse had taken their toll- Mila had never thought to see her mother looking so young. But maybe the Yadeshi had secrets they weren't willing to divulge, even to their human lovers.

Mila faltered a step as the word entered her mind. Lover. She and Jaron weren't fully lovers, but it was only a matter of time.

"Mila!"

She jumped as the Adekhan roared, fumbling the Form. Her training unit was in lines, warming up by going through each movement one by one. She had them memorized to the point where she didn't have to pay much attention.

Demonstrably a bad idea with an Adekhan eyeing her, waiting to pounce.

"Yes, Adekhan."

He moved in front of her, scowling. "Your mind is not in present time. You will give me your mind or you will leave!"

Mila didn't appreciate his attitude. "My mind is my own. The only thing you're entitled to is undivided attention while I'm here. So I'm sorry. I'll focus now."

She dismissed him, and all other thoughts, moving into the Forms fully attuned to her body. The exercise was so different now that she was on a renewed and intensified path to healing. Just in the last few days she'd gained two pounds. Her hair was starting to lose the dull, crackling feel she had to mask with cooking oil to mimic health.

Several hours into training Mila realized the Adekhan's silence after she'd spoken back to him hadn't been anything other than him plotting to make her life miserable.

Had she thought herself healed? Now she knew better.

Mila dropped to her knees after a suicide lap around the giant open air course. The other students could go three laps, but she was still at one.

Physical agony and pride mingled because even a week ago she'd only been able to make it halfway through before collapsing and having to endure Ithann's contemptuous glare.

"Get up, Mila," the Adekhan said.

"Just give me a minute," she said, heart still racing. "I need my heart rate to slow down."

It felt like it would explode from her chest at any minute, and she knew her cardiovascular system couldn't take the strain yet. She'd pushed herself, wanting to prove a point- but that had been stupid.

"You're in poor condition and lazy," Ithann said. "Your mind is lazy. The path the mind sets, the body will follow. If you-"

Mila groaned. "Please, no lectures. You don't know what you're talking about anyway." She hesitated, then shrugged. "I've been sick. I'm recovering, okay? I'll be better in a little while."

His eyes narrowed. They were more of a swampy green today than a true Yadeshi blue. She wondered if he was mixed with another species. Like a reptilian species.

WARRIOR'S VOW

Mila pushed to her feet, bending over to brace her hands on her knees a few seconds before straightening fully. Now that her heart was slowing, she felt the kind of post exercise glow that was a signal of good, rather than poor, health.

"I'm going to recommend you be removed from the program."

Those words caught her attention. She gaped at him a moment, feeling as if a rabid dog had her throat between its maw and was shaking the shit out of her.

"Why would you do that? I'm getting better!"

He braced his legs apart. "Don't like your attitude. And can't imagine you'd make a decent mate for any of our warriors. Better you leave now before we waste more of our time on you."

The words hurt. He didn't know how hard she'd worked, pushing through all the days when she just wanted to crawl up in a ball and stay in bed. But she got up because she needed the money- her mother would need the money- and because even though she'd already decided not to fight death, that didn't mean she had to go pathetically into the night.

"Who decides what is a time waste, Ithann?"

Mila tensed, the icy voice at her back causing the muscles of her abs to tighten. Damn. She hadn't felt him walk up, which meant the Adekhan's verbal blow had thrown her off.

Turning, she put a hand on Jaron's chest, "I don't need you to fight my battles for me."

He didn't even look at her. "It is my right, and my privilege."

"Who says so?"

Jaron looked down. "Isn't that what friends do?"

In his tone was a current, a verbal caress even though no one who didn't know him would hear it. She heard it, and as soon as she began paying attention she felt the upwell of anger inside him. Seething, resentful anger that someone who should be training her was abusing her instead.

Mila hesitated, then stepped aside. She could give him that- a brief submission to his desire to be her knight.

"On the mat," Jaron said, voice soft.

She turned around in time to see Ithann's nasty, disdainful smile. "I should decline out of honor. You are no warrior."

"Then you should have no problem teaching me a lesson."

The men strode to the indoor complex, Mila following at a slower pace and vaguely wondering if she should fetch a snack or some first aid supplies. She hoped Jaron didn't lose too badly- she didn't really have the emotional energy to soothe male ego for the next few days. Though she supposed after all he'd done for her, some soothing was the least way she could repay him.

Gayle ran up, panting. "What's going on?"

"Ithann's being a jerk. Jaron is going to fight him."

"That-" Gayle bit off her words. "I've got to think of something to do to make his life miserable. What a prick."

Mila glanced at her friend, wondering at the perversity of dating someone who one thought was a prick. Just like Gayle- she would think that dynamic intriguing.

The men were headed to an empty mat just as Mila and Gayle entered the gym, the fury swirling around each warrior palpable. People scattered, heads turning as the pair faced each other. Bowed, then stilled for a split second.

And then…

Mila darted forward, skidding to a stop a healthy distance away. The sounds in the gym slowly faded as other Yadeshi and humans realized this fight wasn't training, wasn't practice.

They flowed, the Forms alternating between languid grace and staccato precision. Blow after blow; block, parry. A leap, a kick. Slithering into each other's center to grapple and then breaking away, each man trying to find an advantage. Studying the opponent's strengths and weaknesses.

Ithann's warrior bulk against the leaner, but no less muscular grace of Jaron's form. A study in contrasts. Ithann's sheer power and Jaron's slithering speed, canny ability to anticipate moves. Unlike with Samson's human goons, with Ithann Jaron held nothing back. She heard the murmurs and gasps as people recognized... the *doctor*.

Gayle whistled. "My god, come to mama. I don't supposed you'd be into a-"

"No." Mila cut off Gayle's musing, knowing exactly where her irreverent friend would have gone with that statement.

Mila realized her jaw was open, and laboriously shut it. While Jaron had conducted himself well in the street fight with three humans, it still hadn't occurred to her that he could hold his own against a practicing warrior. Stupid. Where did she think he got his bod from? Bench pressing tongue compressors all day? He must train, albeit in secret. And she understood why- if it was known how good he was, they might reassign him.

"Who authorized this?" a hard female voice asked.

Mila glanced over her shoulder. A tall Yadeshi woman in a long, loose robe like garment, her hair intricately braided, walked into the gym. Though the Yadeshi didn't show age the way humans did, her face seemed timeless.

"No one," Mila replied. "My Adekhan pissed my... boyfriend... off. They're working it out, I guess."

"They're in trouble now," Gayle whispered in Mila's ear, voice gleeful. "This isn't Ithann's day. Ha."

Eyes measured her briefly, before returning to the duel. A sheen of sweat on Jaron's arms. At some point he'd removed the lab coat and revealed his tattooed arms in the same vest as all the warriors.

"This is quite enough," the woman said.

She strode forward, braids swishing around her butt. "Finish it, now."

Her command was a bark. Both men jerked, then moved with renewed fervor. The Adekhan had weight on his side, but Jaron was... fast. In three moves he pinned Ithann to the mat, the Adekhan staring up at him in fury.

"Yield," the woman demanded.

Ithann's incisors flashed then he nodded sharply. Jaron stepped back, bowed.

"Maybe in the future you'll be more constructive in your criticism."

* * *

"Come to my office for a physical," Jaron said, walking towards her.

He'd donned the lab coat again, sliding back into the medical geek persona like it was a second skin. Mila stared at him, unnerved and incredulous.

"I can't just leave- it's the middle of the training day."

"I'm your attending physician. Who here is going to argue with me?"

He hadn't bothered to lower his voice, so the words could be construed as a vague, open challenge. Mila grabbed him by the arm, dragging him from the gym before he could beat up any more of his people. Last thing she needed was a bunch of Adekhana out for her blood. They couldn't touch a doctor- they were considered noncombatant. But they could make Mila's life miserable.

"I thought you didn't fight," she said when they were in the hallway.

He shrugged, pulling his arm away from her. "If you assumed I discontinued all training, that is what I wanted you to assume."

Why, the arrogant sob. Mila stopped, glared at him. "No more fights, Jaron. I have to learn how to take care of myself."

"I agree. But the learning will come in stages I approve. Now Ithann is aware of both your health status- and the need to allow you some leeway- and the need for caution." He smiled, incisors a little extra sharp. "Because, demonstrably, any rude behavior will be chastised."

"Well. Speaking of rude behavior. I guess I'd better tell you the research institute has been hounding me."

The slightly amused, malicious expression on his face shifted. "Explain." No emotion in his tone, eyes hyper focused on her face.

Mila shifted, uncomfortable- maybe her timing was shitty. "Look- do you know something about these people or what? Sometimes I get a vibe from you whenever I bring them up. I know you're in that human alien medical residency program. Has anything come through the grapevine lately?"

"What I have already told you should have been enough, were you an obedient woman," he said, voice even. "However, let me repeat myself. Mila- whatever those people tell you, stay away. Their methodology is aggressive and I don't trust what they're using the data for. Their sponsors-" he stopped talking. "Just cut off all communication. Change your phone number. While you live here at the complex they shouldn't be able to come to your door."

Mila blinked. "It's that serious? I didn't even tell you what they want." And she'd ignore his use of the word *obedient.*

"I know what they want, Mila." His expression was grim. "If you had listened to me and not continued the research, you would not be on their radar now."

"What exactly did your healings do to me, Jaron?"

He didn't answer right away, but began walking. "It alters your genetic structure, makes your cells age slower, become more impervious to attack."

"Oh, my god. Am I turning into an alien?"

He whirled, grabbing her by the arms. "No. You're turning into mine."

She sucked in a breath, unsure of which instinct to obey- the one that wanted to sock him, or the one that wanted to jump his bones.

"Jaron."

They both turned. The female Yadeshi stood several feet away.

"Yanikha," Jaron said.

Yanikha approached, gliding with an unconscious, self-assured authority. Mila glanced between the two Yadeshi, wondering who the woman was.

"Ithann has expressed some concern about trainee Mila's ability to fulfil her training and thus the terms of her contract. He's advised-"

"Do you take advice from Adekhana now?"

Mila tensed. His tone was rude, but the woman only smiled. "It is a valid concern. I've read her file. You're ill, I understand?"

Mila nodded, since Yanikha addressed her. "Yes. I have a rare, terminal cancer. Or I did. Jaron-" she glanced at him, hesitated. Wasn't sure what she should, or should not say.

"I see," the woman said. "Then are the reports of your ill health over exaggerated?"

"At the current time," Jaron said. "And there is every indication her recovery will be complete."

Because of the bond between them, Mila sensed an undercurrent. Her eyes narrowed. "Okay, so what's the subtext I'm missing here?"

Yanikha's head tilted. "He hasn't told you?"

Jaron tensed next to her, and she felt him withdraw. She hadn't realized until then how used she'd become to his mental presence, as subtle as it was.

"Told me what?"

The elder woman waited a beat, but Jaron said nothing. "I don't approve. These things shouldn't be done without the human's full consent."

"What has he done?"

Yanikha met her eyes. "I can sense the bond between you."

Mila wiggled her fingers. "Well, yeah. The healing thingy has created a... connection. He calls it a bond."

"He has not told you what that word truly means. It isn't usually our way to perform it in stages, but... I can see the benefits in this case. He's made you his mate, dear. Not fully. But I suppose that's only a matter of time now."

Mila froze, stunned. "What?"

"You can feel what he feels, can't you? You always know where he is if you concentrate."

She couldn't reply- but the reply was written all over her face. She'd assumed their connection was a simple side effect of the healing... he hadn't said otherwise. Except that one time he'd alluded to- what had he said? Something about her accepting him fully? Damnit, but her brain had been mush even a few days ago.

"Yes," Yanikha said. "When you fully accept the bond, the effects will be magnified."

"I- when I enrolled in the program, the brochure said-"

"We don't put everything in the brochure. By the time you're required to choose a husband, we're hoping you will have already found a natural bond."

She took a deep breath. "Okay, so the 'bond' is good if you're going to have a relationship. "

"My dear, there is no 'going to.' If you bond, it is forever and unescapable. In your case, it appears the if is a when. You're far too close to turn back now."

Mila turned to Jaron. "You weren't going to tell me until it was done."

He returned her glare with arrogant nonchalance. "It isn't really necessary. No one can force a full bond; you have to accept it on your own, as you have been albeit in stages as Yanikha said." He shrugged. "When I take you the point of whether or not I told you will be moot."

8

Mila had the sense to wait until they were alone to chew him out. Moot, her ass. Jaron silenced his clerk with a slashing look as they strode into the office, Mila hard at his heels to the point of subtly pushing him along.

He aimed a glare over his shoulder once or twice, slowing a step so she crashed into his back- and pushed him some more. Stacia sighed and Mila heard her begin to placate patients.

"I don't have time for this, Mila," he said once the door was closed. "I have patients."

She crossed her arms. She felt a little guilty, but not really. "No one out there has anything more serious than a paper cut or Stacia wouldn't have let you get away with shushing her."

He leaned against the desk, crossing his arms. "So what is it?"

"You didn't tell me what you were doing!"

"Does it matter? You needed a cure, I gave you one."

Her teeth clenched. "You didn't mention the cure came with lifetime consequences. Or at least you didn't mention it when I was actually paying attention."

He stared at her, dispassionate. "When does any miracle ever come without strings?"

"Aren't doctors supposed to give full disclosure? Or is this the usual male physician's arrogance, making decisions for a woman because he thinks he knows best?"

"You're a trainee at YETI. You would have to choose a mate anyway. Why not me?"

And she was supposed to endure a lifetime of his cool, seemingly irrefutable logic? Logic that dictated he not consult her on important things?

"I understand," Jaron said. "You think I don't, but I do. But my higher imperative- besides respecting your free will- is to preserve life. That is my first vow, Mila. Even if the preservation of your life is against your will."

Her shoulders slumped. She heard the hard line in his voice, even as the true ring of his words told her he was utterly convinced he was correct.

"Fine, Jaron. But don't expect me to ever really trust you."

His eyes narrowed. "You have centuries to learn to trust me. Right now all I want is your vow."

"Vow? Wait- centuries? What the hell?"

"I want to fully mate. I want a life with you, Mila."

"Can we go back to the centuries thing?"

He straightened from the desk, arms resting at his sides. "I've courted you slowly over the last few months. Given you time. I'm old enough to know when a connection has the potential to be something enduring." He waited a beat as she absorbed his words. "Are you?"

She took a deep breath. "We have issues to work out- your high handedness being one. Tell me more about my centuries."

He smiled, and the genuine warmth softened her anger. "No. Now go play."

* * *

"Can we talk?"

Mila turned her head as she left the office. Her mother stood a few feet away, arms wrapped around herself.

Approaching, Mila gave Ayita a hug. "It will be alright, Mama. Jaron's taking care of you, right?"

"Giving you a break," her mother said after pulling away from the hug. Ayita's brow was furrowed, worry lines on her forehead. "I should be taking care of you."

"I'm a big girl."

"He told me."

Mila's smile evaporated. "He had no right."

"You should have told me. I never would have let you go through with that." Ayita blinked, a sheen in her eyes. "Do you think I want your death on my shoulders, too?"

Mila jerked away, stung. "I was trying to make sure you were taken care of!"

"Well, stop that stupid shit," Ayita retorted. "It isn't your job to fix my issues, Mimi. I'm the parent- I've been a shitty one, but I'm still your mother. I want to focus on you." Ayita shook her head. "There's something about this place that clears the head. Or maybe I was finally ready to start healing for real."

"Samson is gonna want you to pay the tab."

Ayita grimaced. "I'll talk to him. I know some shit that will 'pay my tab' for me."

"Ma-"

"Don't worry about me, Mila." Ayita's lips pursed. "Though if you go back to the apartment, I could really use my house shoes. The pink fluffy ones I've had for-"

"Ten years." Mila grimaced. "Gross. Okay, Ma."

* * *

She returned to her training in a better spirit, feeling as if some of the issues between her and Jaron, between her and Ayita, were on the path to resolution. Everything wouldn't be perfect overnight, but it felt like a new start, the breaking of a destructive cycle. Finally.

After training she left the complex, wanting to gather some more of their belongings. They had until the end of the month paid up in the apartment, and Mila had a feeling Jaron was going to ask her to move into his suite permanently.

She wasn't sure how she felt about the idea- the complex was perfectly fine, with all the up to date amenities and technology. The living quarters were comfortable and even the common areas were nice, but she wanted a place of her own. Maybe she could convince him to pick out something off complex. Would Ayita want to move in as well?

"Mila."

Mila turned as she finished locking the apartment door, shoulders prickling. "Rebecca, what are you doing here?"

The doctor strode down the hallway, low heeled shoes clicking. She smiled, brisk and friendly.

"I'd like to talk to you. Can we go for a cup of coffee?"

Mila shrugged. "I don't see any point. I've already decided-"

"No, no, I understand. I won't ask you about the program again, but I've been attending you for a while now. I'd like to make sure everything is okay."

Sincerity shone from her eyes. Mila relaxed, although reluctantly. A doctor's imperative to heal she understood.

"Okay. But I don't have much time, I have to get back to training."

"Of course."

The vintage building didn't boast a working elevator so they walked down three flights of stairs, Rebecca chatting amicably while Mila made noncommittal noises.

Once in the parking lot, Mila glanced at the street to see if the bus was coming.

"I have a van," Rebecca said.

Mila turned towards her, about to reply when she realized the doctor was no longer chattering, and no longer smiling.

Hands grabbed her upper arms. "Come with us, ma'am," a male voice said.

She fought, of course. It was broad daylight, so someone should have noticed the noise she made, but... yeah, right. No one would want to involve themselves. Not with a government looking vehicle and uniformed goon scuffling with one skinny woman known to be living on assistance with a drug addicted mother.

A prick in her arm and her vision went fuzzy, mind turning to a kind of mush.

"Nice skills," the goon said after throwing her in the back of the van. His voice came from a tunnel. Mila sat very still to calm the spinning in her head, vaguely realizing they must have drugged her.

He settled on the bench opposite her, untroubled by her glaring. "They told us you have some of the fancy training from the Blue Men. Still a beginner, huh?"

"This is illegal," she said, forcing herself to think coherently. Her head began to ache. "As soon as my- attending physician at YETI finds out I'm missing, they'll come looking for me."

Good shrugged. "Wouldn't worry about it. Good security at the complex."

The man had the nerve to unwrap a sandwich and begin eating, ignoring her by all appearances. Mila knew better. He was watching. He just knew she had nowhere to go. The van was empty of anything she could use as a weapon, not even a pencil or a furniture strap. She didn't have the strength to pick him up and bash his head against the metal bench- she seen some of the female warriors make moves like that, but they were the rocked up Yadeshi women with years of conditioning.

Mila waited, feeling her mind clear in minute increments. So. Whatever he'd injected her with wasn't meant to last long- just long enough. And then it occurred to her, as she was trying to imagine Jaron's reaction when he realized she was missing.

They were almost bonded.

* * *

They took her through intake almost as if she were a regular patient.

The only differences were the wrist restraints, and the basement.

"You know, basement laboratories have a really bad reputation," Mila said to Rebecca. "I think I prefer the top floor accommodations."

The doctor ignored her, scanning them through security. Goon said nothing either, right at her shoulder. Not touching, but close enough that she sure as hell wasn't gonna try and make a run for it.

At least not yet.

Her head pounded and beads of sweat broke through the skin at her temples. For the third time she focused, stretching her mind out towards Jaron. And yelled at the top of her mental lungs. She didn't really know what she was doing, of course, but she'd seen movies. Didn't telepathic people just think in images and emotions at each other?

But each time she tried, her skull split from the pain. She gasped, trying to keep her breathing even, but the last effort caused her heart to speed up and her breath to quicken as if she were running. Rebecca did glance at her then, frowning.

"Are you ill?"

They went through another set of clear doors until they arrived at a section of the lab that held cubicles, each enclosed with the plexiglass walls. The tiny rooms were equipped with hospital beds and a single chair. A side table large enough for a tray and a flat screen television. Several of them were occupied.

"So are they all here of their own free will?" Mila asked.

Rebecca put her hand on Mila's forehead. Mila jerked away glaring.

"Your temperature is elevated," Rebecca said. "Let's get you settled in and order something to eat and drink so you can relax. We don't need your system flooded with stress hormones."

"Yeah, can't have that," Mila muttered.

She cast her gaze around, desperately trying to think of a plan, but nothing came to mind. So much for her months of training. She turned her mind on the guard, but as soon as she reached out, the pain sent her stumbling. Goon caught her, half dragging, half assisting her into her observation cell.

Okay. She'd have to bide her time for a minute.

Dimly, Mila heard Rebecca speak in docotorese, ordering various tests and equipment as well as food.

"We don't have to begin right away, Mila," the doctor said, voice distant. "Rest for now."

* * *

Her pain struck him, the bolt so unexpected that if he'd been wielding anything sharp, someone would have been seriously hurt. Jaron controlled his involuntary hunch and immediately traced her mind along their fading link. Images flooded him, chaotic hazy frames a toddler would send. Or an untrained human with potential. He took each image and processed the available data, picking out the details until the slides formed a cohesive whole.

Hands on his shoulders, his arms, lifting, throwing him into a vehicle. A short, tense trip and a walk inside a building he recognized. Jaron grit his teeth, strangling his anger since it would only distort the pictures. Her mind flickered out several times and

Jaron could only wait, frustration a blood-curdling roar of impatience inside him. He was the receiver; he could only hope she would reach out to him again.

She did, enough times that he understood what was happening.

Jaron rose from a crouch he hadn't known he'd fallen in, shedding the lab coat and striding from the office towards the training grounds. He would need warriors. He would raze that research building to the ground.

* * *

Mila figured the mind was a muscle. And since she didn't believe in spooky things, whatever she was doing to infiltrate other's thoughts was brain based. So she took it easy, especially when she dabbed a single drop of blood from her nostril. She'd rest, remain cooperative, let her temperature go down so she didn't inadvertently blow her brain up.

But she watched the staff move from station to station, and tried to determine what the security response would be if she were able to escape her cell. Should she wait for Jaron or make a go for it? There was no way of knowing if he'd even heard her.

She whispered his name, not reaching out, not doing anything to strain herself, but this time an awareness flooded her mind, settling over her like a familiar blanket. No words- she wasn't skilled enough for words. But a sense of reassurance, and grim determination.

Mila smiled and settled back onto the thing hospital pillows. Her alien was on his way.

* * *

Ithann came with him.

"We can't destroy the building or the people," the Adekhan said. "There will be enough repercussions simply from extracting her."

"Kidnapping is illegal."

"No killing."

Jaron knew the Adekhan was right. He would... hold back. But only for Mila's sake, so her life wouldn't be disrupted by the aftermath of her rescue. He would raze the building to the ground- but he'd do enough damage to make a point.

9

She pushed the button at her bedside. Goon appeared a few minutes later, face tight.

"What?" he growled.

"I don't drink cow's milk," she said, indicating the boxed chocolate milk an orderly had brought her with her tray of lunch. "Do you have almond or coconut?"

He stared. "We have water."

Mila considered, head tilted. Then she smiled, and very gently suggested, "I think you'd like to go to the closest store and get me some chocolate almond milk."

He stared one long moment, then turned on his heels, shoulders tense with annoyance. Mila carefully extricated her mind from his, his aggravation dissipating as he left the lab.

So. Goon would be easy enough to influence.

Mila waited, rested, observed. As Jaron's presence intensified- she assumed that meant he was getting closer- she conserved her strength. She knew he wouldn't come alone. That wouldn't be the most effective strategy. The tendrils of his anger warmed the base of her spine, warning her that this time, he might not behave with cool logic, however. And this was the time she needed his intellect the most.

Rather than actively shoving images down their mental pipeline, she imagined each mental frame as a bubble, and let it gently drift along their connection. This enabled her to feed him information without straining herself. Not as effective, but less taxing.

She dozed a bit because she was tired and because there wasn't much else she could do but wait. If she tried to break free prematurely, it would only tip the staff off to expect something, perhaps increase her security or put her in restraints.

WARRIOR'S VOW

And then Jaron was there, in her mind, demanding she prepare herself. Mila sat up, grinning.

* * *

Jaron recognized the man from Mila's hazy images.

"There," he said to Ithann. "The guard who accompanied her."

There were eight warriors with them, more than enough to subdue a medical facility. They'd already checked that the security here was unarmed-stun phasors didn't count, no Yadeshi warrior worth his or her training would be taken down by a rudimentary stun gun.

"What's that in his hand?" Ithann asked

Jaron's eyes narrowed. "A beverage."

The Adekhan stepped away from the building that shielded them from direct sight. "We follow him in. He'll lead us to where she's being held." Ithann paused. "Will she be any help?"

"You'll find out."

They approached all at once, not seeing any point in attempting stealth in the middle of the day- eight tall, blue warriors plus one crazy human woman.

Jaron frowned at Gayle. "*No* killing, trainee Gayle."

She grinned, flipping her long blue braids and streaking towards the facility.

"Yeah, yeah, no killing," she shouted. "Don't worry, I called my father already. He's rich, and he has lawyers!"

* * *

An alarm sounded just as Goon handed Mila her chocolate almond milk. Staff jerked and began shouting directives, shutting down computers and beginning evacuation.

She grabbed his mind as he turned. "Open all the secured entrances, and stand down."

This was harder to pull off. He fought the command, naturally- having him go fetch her a drink was annoying, but not threatening and was in line with the imperative to provide her lunch. This was different.

Mila gasped, her body slow heating like a furnace. "Open secured entrances, and stand down."

His will broke, finally. He was just human after all, and she'd had months of alteration thanks to her sly almost mate. Goon ran to do her bidding, several staff crying out in alarm as he punched in codes to open the sliding doors.

Mila followed him, waving a cheery thanks as he watched her walk out, brow furrowed. She dabbed at her nose, grin faltering as each step became a drag through mud. Dream-like mud, where the world around her began to haze and it felt as if she was moving each limb a bare inch at a time.

"Jaron," she whispered, leaning against a wall. "I think I broke my brain."

The sounds of shouting reached her ears. Heavy running feet and several thumps. She worried, for a brief moment, that the Yadeshi might break the treaty by permanently injuring or even killing someone, but realized they were skilled enough warriors to subdue a bunch of techs with minimal force.

The doors at the end of the wide, sterile hallway slid open; sort of anti-climactic. There was no crashing, no dramatic leaping of her rescuers armed with light swords and flowing hair into her place of imprisonment.

It was almost disappointing.

Jaron strode down the hallway, eating ground in the way Yadeshi did by making it look like they were barely moving. Then blue braids appeared, Gayle making her entrance with a series of cartwheels.

"Hey, girl! Thanks for the real time training op," Gayle shouted. "And we'll owe my dad a favor. He's gonna clean this little breach of entry mess up."

Mila's heart sank. The last thing she wanted was a rich, High Tier entrenched politician with his eye on her. But maybe it was a good thing- if it was standard practice to kidnap research patients, this place needed to be shut down.

"Hey," Mila said through her splitting headache.

Jaron reached her, but stopped a hands width away.

"Are you well?" he asked.

And Mila realized he wouldn't embarrass her in front of the other warriors by implying she needed his help. She straightened from her crouch against the wall, nodding carefully.

"It's all good," she said.

"Right on," Gayle said. "Hey, I'm feeling faint from all the action, can I lean on you?"

Trust Gayle to make it look like *she* was leaning on *Mila* when it was the other way around. No one was fooled, but it was a dignified way to save face.

They made it back to the complex in silence. Mila's entire body trembling by the time they arrived. Jaron lifted her in his arms without a word, or a protest from Gayle.

"The only thing that will help you right now is food and rest," he said, keeping his voice quiet, so as not to cause her more pain.

But even breathing made her head hurt right now.

"Mila, if we share energy again, you'll heal quickly."

She heard the but in his voice and stirred as he laid her on the bed. She waited, though, closing her eyes and listening as he moved to the communicator, ordered a meal to his specifications- lots of carbs and quality protein. When he entered the sleeping area again and sat on the bed, Mila reached for his hand.

"But?" she asked. She opened her eyes to watch his face as he replied.

"You're close to accepting the bond. If you want to delay, then it's better if we don't."

Mila sighed. "For someone so smart, you can be incredibly dense."

She pushed herself into a sitting position, arms trembling, and lifted her shirt over her head. He watched, still, as she unclasped her bra.

"Healing?" she asked. Truth was, she didn't feel up to much more but she could at least enjoy *something*.

Jaron removed his shirt vest and stretched out next to her, sliding an arm around her waist and pulling her on top of him so their chests mashed together. Mila closed her eyes, resting her head in the hollow of his collarbone. Hands slid down her back, cupped her buttocks underneath her leggings and squeezed her flesh. Lights behind her eyes and the tingly warmth that always accompanied when they shared energy.

This time was no different; his essence flooded her and she felt stronger. But... then it cut off, leaving her hungry, wanting more.

Mila opened her eyes. "You stopped."

"When you are ready for the full bond, I won't."

She half pushed up, staring down at him, her hair falling around her shoulders and into his face. "Why not now?"

His eyes glowed. "No. When you are completely well."

Mila shifted so she was straddling him, his hardness rubbing against her. She undulated her hips, not feeling one whit of remorse when his eyes closed as if in pain. Hands around her waist halted her movements.

Jaron flipped her off him, pressing a kiss to her forehead as he rose from the bed. "Rest, Mila. You can seduce me tomorrow."

* * *

She tried. She really did. Jaron was having none of it.

Mila didn't know what he was waiting for, but after a few days of playing the cat and mouse game, she resumed her training.

"What's eating you?" Gayle asked. "Don't get me wrong- whatever it is, it's made you sharper. Your reflexes are improving."

Mila parried a strike, assessed an opening left by Gayle's miscalculation and scored a blow to her best friend's ribs. She pulled most of her weight right before the kick landed, so it wouldn't bruise that bad.

Gayle swore, and renewed her offensive Forms. "Alright, you wanna be a big girl," the tall woman said, with narrowed eyes. "Let's be big girls."

It was cheesy as hell, but a grin tugged Mila's lips. She engaged with renewed vigor, wishing she had Jaron's mind, his experience. The fight was a dance, but at her level it was still a broken dance. Inadvertently she reached along their bond- the *unfinished bond.* And tapped into…. something. His knowledge, his strength, his experience. Whatever it was, Jaron's essence flooded her and her limbs straightened, her gait smoothing to a warrior like gracefulness.

Gayle's offensive Forms faltered, deteriorating into defensive Forms. She faltered, giving ground. Mila pushed, earning every inch, breath coming rapidly.

"Mila-" Gayle panted.

The song of battle filled her ears, the sound of an enemy's broken cries as they were about to be-

"*Mila!*"

His essence vanished and she stumbled, falling to one knee, marrow suddenly nothing more than gravy. Jaron's angry concerned presence at her back and Ithann glaring.

"Oh god," Mila breathed. "What *was* that?"

"Are you injured?"

She thought Jaron was talking to her but when she glanced up he was crouched next to Gayle, who'd thrown herself spread eagled on the ground. Mila glared at his back. She didn't begrudge her best friend medical attention, but did he have to sound so concerned?

Ithann strode up, eyes fixed on Jaron. "Don't touch-"

Jaron's head jerked up and he shot Ithann a hot, irritated glance. "I'm a doctor."

"I don't care."

Jaron rose and backed away. "Fine. Bring her to the infirmary when you have some sense."

"I'm good," Gayle groaned. "I'm missing out on all my childhood whoopings anyway."

Mila bit her lip, twisting her arms behind her back. "G? We good?"

"Yeah, girl, go get a drink or something, I'm alright."

Jaron approached, eyes hard as he examined Mila. She returned his glare with one of her own.

"You aren't worried about me?" she asked.

"You were never in any danger." He took her arm, pulling her with him. "You will have to be trained. Soon. You're stronger than you should be at this stage."

"Well, dandy. Train me then. But you've been avoiding me for-"

"I haven't been avoiding you." He stopped just inside the complex, pushing her against a wall, caging Mila with both arms as he stared down at her. "I've been giving you time to heal."

"Well, I'm healed! I think you just have second thoughts and you won't man up and tell me. You're flaky."

His eyes widened in outrage. "Your accusations are irrational. Furthermore-"

"Children."

Mila recognized the warm, feminine voice. She looked over Jaron's shoulder as he straightened- though he didn't release Mila.

"Yanikha."

Yanikha came forward. "I heard about the incident. I'm pleased."

Mila blinked. "Pleased?"

The woman looked around Jaron, smiling. "Yes. It is good you have so strong a bond that it has cultivated a very valuable latent ability. And the bond not every fully consummated."

She felt her cheeks heat. Mila knew what consummated meant. How the hell did these people know Jaron still hadn't slept with her? She didn't like that shit. Made her look like she wasn't... desirable.

Okay. So she was skinnier than she should be, and a bit mouthy. Clumsy…

"Mila." He was looking at her, the slant of his shoulders agitated. "Stop that."

"What?"

"I can feel what you're thinking and I don't like it. Stop it."

"I think you two have things to discuss," Yanikha said. "Jaron, you are correct. Both of you report in two days and we will determine the extra instruction required. And Mila, there is no longer any question regarding your fitness to be here."

Mila snorted as the woman walked away. Of course there wasn't. She'd almost rescued herself, beat up Gayle, did a new mind thingy that turned her into super ninja… of course they would want to keep her around now.

"I think it's time for our talk," Jaron said.

Mila looked at him. He said the word 'talk'… not like the word talk. She licked her lips. "Talk talk? Or *talk?*"

He shifted, hips pressing against her, erection obvious. "You may be right. If you are strong enough to defeat

Gayle... perhaps I am being overprotective. And I have waited long enough."

"We. *We've* waited. All the 'I' stuff gives the wrong impression."

He stepped back, held out his hand. She clasped it without hesitation and followed him to their quarters.

10

He led her through the hallways silently, hand wrapped firmly around her own. Mila almost asked him to slow down, but could sense he was focused on one thing.

Inside the apartment, Mila tugged away. He whirled, backing her against the wall with a speed that took her breath. His eyes were hot, expression almost, but not quite, cruel.

"Have you changed your mind?" he asked.

"No." She stared up at him, heart beating fast. "But… you aren't going to go all berserk or anything are you?"

His arm slid around her waist, the other hand burrowing in the hair at her nape. He tugged her head back and captured her lips. Lengthened incisors drew a drop of blood and he suckled the liquid, hold tightening almost painfully.

"Are you strong enough to take all of me?" he asked, voice hoarse.

His desire flooded her system, mingling and amplifying her own. And she went from uncomfortably horny and understandably eager to madly, insatiably desiring him. Mila cried out, arching her pelvis against his and he laughed, low and dark.

"This is what I feel every waking moment."

It took her two tries to speak. "You've been shielding it from me."

"Yes." The word was a sibilant hiss. "No more."

She reached up, wrapping her hands around his neck. "No more. I want you. Now."

He dragged her into his room, holding her up when her feet would have tangled with his own and tripped her. Mila didn't care. She wanted to be ravished- she wanted to do the ravishing. Jaron lifted her and tossed her on the bed, stomach first, his body pressing full length against hers. She turned her head, bracing her arms to hold his weight.

There were no niceties- he tore the leggings from her body, taking her underwear with them and his teeth, his hands were on her ass. Biting, massaging. Nudging her thighs apart, he licked his way to her crevice before pulling back just enough.

"Get on your knees," he said, moving off her so she could comply.

Instead she rolled off the bed, taking her shirt and tugging it over her head. She turned and stood before him, naked. His eyes flashed a brilliant, star fueled blue, drinking in her nudity. She stretched for him, thrusting her breasts and spreading her legs. She'd gained weight in the last several days, her ribs filling out and the gap between her thighs almost gone. Soon she would even have the gentle roundness of her tummy back.

"I want a baby from you," she said.

He inhaled abruptly. "I'll give you one. Come here."

Mila closed the distance between them and his hands slid around her waist, down to cup her buttocks.

"But first," he said. "You need to gain weight."

"First we need to fuck."

He laughed, and when he bent his head as if to kiss her again she shook her head, dropping to her knees.

"I want to hear you scream," she said, and took the waistband of his loose trousers, tugging the pants down- more gently than he with her- and exposed him. "Take off the shirt, blue man."

He discarded the vest, stripping for her slowly, making a show of revealing the sculpted chest, hard abs. His skin was deep azure all over, but his hairless groin area shimmered, as if the cock was magical. Mila grinned. She was certain he'd like to think so, anyway.

Mila grasped the base of his cock, eyeing it with delight and trepidation. She knew her pussy was designed to push out something at least as big as a baby- but would it work the other way around?

Her hand just barely fit around the width, so she began with leaning forward to taste the glistening bead of pre cum on the tip. His rounded mushroom head was smooth, the taste honey sweet. It jerked in her hold and she almost snatched her hand back as the heat radiating from the cock escalated, nearly searing her.

"Fuck," she swore. "I'll have a furnace inside me."

And he was hot inside her mouth, almost like too hot tea. She slowly fitted her lips around him, mostly using her tongue to lick and caress his hard shaft. If anything, he swelled more, liquid seeping into her mouth. She moved back and forth on the first inch of him unable to open her jaws any wider.

He groaned, hands tangling in her hair. "My heat will increase until we come," he said. "I won't waste my seed in your mouth. Not this time."

Jaron pulled her to her feet, roughly so her chest smashed against his torso. He pressed against her stomach, both promise and warning. Lifting her by the waist, Jaron walked backwards, Mila's legs wrapping around him, opening for him.

They tumbled onto the bed, Jaron careful to land most of his weight on his arms on either side of her head. She reached between their bodies and grabbed him again, running her hand up and down the silky jewel toned skin.

Holding her eyes while she guided his cock towards her entrance, Jaron pressed inside a small space at a time. Mila bit her lip against the urge to impale herself, reining in impatience to allow her body to adjust to the huge invasion.

Slowly, stretching her body even with the aid of her moist arousal, he sank inside her.

He kissed her. "Are you well?"

One breath, two. "Yes."

Mila wrapped her hands around his biceps and arched her hips, forcing him the rest of the way inside her. Their mingled hisses of pleasure, the heat of him inside her. He slid out, pushed back in, each time easier than the next until a steady rhythm built. Mila's hips pumped; she wanted him harder, deeper. Under her fingers his markings flared, much like during a healing but brighter. Rapidly the tattoos began to split, slithering around and down his arms, the duplicates slithering over her hands and up to rest, lock, around her upper arms.

Triumph in Jaron's face, eyes a brilliant blue even as Mila's orgasm crested, her body stiffening from the intense, shocking completion. A moment later he followed, hot seed flooding her womb. She felt him inside her, the bond strengthened, a mental snap into place and for a moment his mind was hers; hers his.

And she felt... love. Not a comfortable love, but the fierce, focused, intense desire to cherish, protect- take and possess.

Her legs slithered to the bed, body spent. Jaron's head rested next to hers as his heat slowly faded. He still didn't remove himself from inside her and as the aftershocks of pleasure began to wane, Mila winced.

He lifted his head immediately. "Are you hurt?"

She smiled, wry. "I won't be the first woman who's a little sore after a good fucking."

Jaron's narrowed eyes studied her face, then he raised a hand to caress her cheek. "You accepted the bond. You know what that means."

Her eyes rolled. "Yeah, yeah. I'm yours."

"It means I love you," he said quietly.

Mila froze. She knew it, of course. But to hear the words, so freely spoken... "I love you, too. You're my best friend. Well, my best guy friend. I mean, Gayle is like-"

He smiled, sardonic. "I understand." Lightning fast, he cupped her mound. "As long as you both understand this is all for me."

Mila's eyes widened. "Oh, yeah. I understand."

"Good."

And as he began to harden again inside her, Mila swallowed. "Again?"

A small, malicious smile curved his lips in reaction to the squeak in her voice. "Of course again. And again, and again."

All night long.

EPILOGUE

Mila felt strong. She stretched, twisting in the locker room mirror to admire the sleek lines of her toned arms and shoulders, the full curvature of breast and hip and thigh. And ass. Yegads... the ass.

"Isn't preening wonderful?" Gayle asked, binding her long braids into a bun at the nape of her neck. She dropped into a crouch, performed a series of quick punches.

Mila rolled her eyes. "Let's get this over with."

They'd waited a full three months before deciding to tie up Ayita's loose end. She'd tagged Gayle to accompany her instead of Jaron because she didn't really want anyone to die. Besides, they didn't need the big blue men to come with them and if Jaron came, then Ithann would want to come as well.

"What are you doing here?" Samson asked with a scowl, bleary eyed, when they banged on his door.

Mila strolled past him into his house, Gayle on her heels looking around with bright eyed interest. "You should really try and get to bed at a decent time, Sam. You don't look hot."

He slammed the door. Mila turned, adjusting her stance, ever so slightly.

"Slamming doors is rude," Gayle said.

"Who the fuck is you?" He squinted. "Hey, aren't you-"

"No. I get that all the time. Must be the hair."

He tugged up the waistband of his drooping pants. His white tank didn't look entirely clean, but then it must have been his maid's day off.

"What do you want, Mila? You here to pay the tab?"

Mila crossed her arms, balancing on the balls of her feet. "I'm here to make you an offer you can't refuse." He laughed, but she ignored him. "Ayita is broke. I'm broke-"

"That's a lie. I heard you was messin' around with them aliens, girl. They got money."

"They have muscle," Gayle corrected.

"Yeah? Where is it? Not here." Samson pulled a communicator out of his pocket and tapped a few buttons.

Mila snapped her fingers in his face. "Don't get sidetracked. What I'm going to do is make six monthly payments in an amount that will equal one fourth of what Ayita owes you. In return, I won't rat your ass out for being an unlicensed dealer."

He stilled. "You wanna watch your mouth. Your Mama will be back here sooner or later and I'll take your disrespect out on her."

The threat didn't faze her. "My mother will *never* be back here- and she's somewhere you won't be able to touch her."

She didn't have to tell him Ayita was in the beginning stages of her own Happily Ever After. Mila hoped it worked out for her. It was about time, after all.

"You can get out of my house," Samson said. "I'll take full payment in cash, or ass. One or the other and you have a week." He stopped. "You know what, forget that shit. Give me my money now."

Mila heard the back door open and bang shut and the sound of feet on the creaking wood floors. A moment later the hallway was cramped by four of his enforcers. Mila shifted so her back was to the wall but she could keep an eye on Samson and his goons. Gayle did likewise, insouciant grin even brighter.

"Oooh- I love parties," her friend said.

"Looks like," Samson said. "So what's it gonna be? Cash or ass? Same deal I give your Mama. It's only fair."

Mila smiled without amusement. Poor man.

He'd just pissed her off.

If you'd like to know how the story continues, from Gayle's POV, swipe forward for Warrior's Mate.

EMMA ALISYN

SNEAK PEEK...

WARRIOR'S MATE

WARRIORS OF YEDAHN #3

A Dark Alien Prince + his unquenchable desire x his insatiable thirst = a warrior willing to defy a galaxy to claim his mate.

1

Ithann's almond shaped eyes, deceptively pretty with their long lashes, stared at Gayle with chilly malice. She honed in on those lashes, well suited to the unearthly lines of his face, because the tiniest flick of a lash was his absolute only tell. But no luck this time- he watched her as she watched him, his stern lips quirking in a mocking smile at her meager attempt to best him. He beckoned, an insolent flick of his fingers, inviting her to try his defenses.

She wasn't stupid. As good as she was among the students, and even among civilian humans, she was no match for a fully trained and blooded warrior. This fight was child's play to him- not so much for her, since she was the one getting her ass kicked.

It was his job, after all, to give her exactly what she'd signed up for when enrolling at the Academy for training as a human warrior-bride candidate in the Yadeshi military. Innocuously referred to as YETI, the Yadeshi-Earth Training Institute merrily recruited unsuspecting women to provide alien warriors with fresh... mates. But they were all students first, and the best of the alien warriors, the *Adekhan*, were their instructors. *Adekhan* Ithann took his duty in training the future mothers of his race seriously. He didn't have to enjoy it so much, though.

"Yield," Ithann said. "It's time for my tea."

The alien bastard didn't drink tea- he must have been studying colloquialisms again. Gayle shifted into Third Form, ignoring his taunt and the snickers from some of the watching students. She'd finally learned not to respond to his verbal insults or the noise in the tiny weiner gallery, the former delivered with masterful timing and designed to elicit the optimal level of ire. She didn't fight well when angry- the *Adekhan* knew her weakness and exploited it shamelessly.

Besides, she didn't have the breath left over for speech. It was all she could do just to remain upright. Her teacher, and would be lover, offered her no more quarter than he would any other *aja'eko*. In fact, the tattooed blue fiend offered her even less. But if he fucked like he fought, when she finally gave in to the inevitable, Gayle fully expected a wild ride.

Ithann's nostrils flared, the pale blue of his irises brightening to white. He *moved*, cutting through her guard and disabling her defenses. In seconds she was flat on her stomach, arms twisted behind her in a hold as the heavily muscled warrior leaned over her, mouth close to her ear. His long hair bushed the sides of her cheek.

"I know what you're thinking," he murmured in her ear. "Your lust betrays you."

"Why don't you do something about it then?" She didn't bother lowering her voice.

A quick, hidden nip on her ear, the bite painful enough that Gayle yelped.

"I have plans, *aja'eko*. I'll repay you for the past several weeks of taunting soon. I promise you."

She was too smart not to be nervous.

* * *

"He said that?" Mila asked, wiping the sweat from her face with a towel.

Ithann had dismissed the training group after their match, and strode away without another look or word for Gayle.

Gayle grinned. "Yeah, I think I've worn him down."

Mila snorted. "You just *think* you're the one doing the wearing. We're talking about a Yadeshi warrior, girl. Their plans have plans. That have plans. And little baby plans."

"Yeah? Well, the result will be the same. Hot rabid sex in the locker room shower and then-"

"Bonding marks? Hello, Yadeshi warrior?"

"Details." Gayle winced. She wanted the alien, liked the alien, even thought he'd make a decent enough long term partner. By the terms of her admission to the Academy, she had to choose- or allow herself to be chosen by- a Yadeshi warrior to mate. But bonding tattoos? She wasn't nearly ready to go there yet. "I think I prefer to just stick with the hot rabid sex in the shower for now."

Mila snorted, rifling through her gym bag for a fresh change of clothes. "Okay. We'll see how this turns out, anyway. Have you told your parents?"

Gayle sighed. "I will. Eventually. Maybe even tonight."

"Family dinner?"

"Don't sound so sympathetic."

Mila patted Gayle's shoulder as she passed to go to the showers. "Gourmet meal made from real food and not synthetics, plush High Tier surroundings? I don't feel all *that* sorry for you."

* * *

Gayle wouldn't have felt sorry for herself, either. Her parents had had the dining room remodeled while she'd bunked in the Academy dorms over the last week. She couldn't stop staring at the blue-and-white glass tiles, the intricate pattern hand laid by an artisan. All the old, overblown furniture gone, replaced by pieces made of warm honey wood—real wood, not fabricated. The painting on the wall she recognized because her parents had also overpaid for a useless private school education.

The paintings weren't replications.

Gayle's fingers clenched the delicate flute of her water glass. "So, do the taxpayers know that you just spent close to a mil in credits on your dining room when there are talks the government won't be able to fund food vouchers this quarter?"

"Really, Abigail," her mother said, setting her fork down with an abrupt clink. "We don't discuss politics at the table."

That was a lie. They simply didn't discuss politics that were an implicit criticism to the High Tier lifestyle at the table. Her elegant, expertly coiffed mother lifted a finger to have the salad course cleared away.

"We used our private funds, of course," her father said, sipping his wine. "We'd never utilize tax dollars for personal projects."

"Why not take a salary cut? Your salary is paid for by the people, which means the people indirectly funded a dining room remodel. The old one was fine." Gayle glared as her mother opened her mouth to protest. "It's fine, Mother. Why don't you find something useful to do with your time rather than trying to replicate the latest *Modern Housekeeping* spread?"

Miranda's dark eyes iced over. "I'll thank you to alter your tone of voice. You're fortunate that the taxpayers provide so generously for your father, who works hard on their behalf, and affords you the opportunity to pursue your leisure activities."

"I'm a student at the Academy, it's not a leisure sport."

"Really. And all the other women who are enrolled aren't Low and Middle Tier women with no education and little means, forced to engage in war-play on the off chance they might catch the eye of a non-human."

Gayle stood. She wasn't going to sit and bandy words with her parents. She had work to do.

"Abigail, sit down," her father said, his voice steely.

She glanced at him. The tone was a rare one that he only trotted out in important circumstances. She wasn't a teenager anymore—was several years past her majority, but she sat, eyes narrowing.

"We'll have to do something about her hair, of course," Miranda declared. "The color is... modern, I suppose, but the braids aren't really in the current fashion. Really, Gayle, why do you insist on—"

"What's going on?" Gayle speared her father with her own steely look.

The family remained silent as servers brought in the next course. Gayle ate her soup, more because her body needed the fuel than because she was hungry. And though the meals at the Academy were top notch, they were still prepared in a cafeteria. Her parents' private chef would have been appalled to see how Gayle had been eating lately. Everything very hearty, seasoned nicely, but very plain. The kind of food soldiers would eat.

Gayle realized her internal dialogue sounded like her mother talking, and stared down at her soup bowl with displeasure. Soup crafted purely for the sake of culinary art, and not to provide the maximum amount of nutrition available while stretching a meager food voucher.

She wanted to push it aside in protest, but that would defeat the purpose. A hungry person would never waste food just for principle. She attacked the soup with gusto.

Her mother noticed. "If you're that hungry, dear, I can have a snack sent up to your room before you retire."

"What's the deal, Dad?" Gayle asked the man sipping his soup while he swiped reports on his tablet.

He darkened the screen and turned his attention back to his only daughter. "Abigail, we aren't pleased by the media coverage given your participation in the events at the research facility. Several offers we received for a marriage alliance were withdrawn."

What wonderful news. "Good."

"I, of course, admire your sense of civic duty—though misplaced—as our family has its root in community organizing, but your mother and I feel we've allowed you to pursue this hobby far too long."

"*Hobby?*"

"You don't need the Academy," Miranda said. "You're neither poor, nor lacking options. In fact, your presence takes away a slot from some unfortunate woman who really needs it. You're slumming, dear, and it's time to come home and take up your responsibilities to your family."

She knew where this was going. Had expected it for a while. "You want me to marry."

"We think it's best. There are several choices that would bring the family invaluable political and business connections."

"And what am I supposed to do after I get married?"

Her mother stared, unblinking. "Whatever you want. There will be a household to maintain, social events to plan. Children to raise. If you marry a politician, you'll be expected to engage in some form of public service, of course."

Gayle sighed. "I'm not going to marry. You guys can just get that thought right out of your heads."

"I'm afraid I'm going to insist, Abigail," her father said. "You're embarrassing us with this Academy nonsense. I've indulged you far too long."

"Has everyone forgotten that I'm an adult? This whole conversation reads like you're talking to a rebellious teenager."

"Either you exit the Academy, and find a suitable spouse, or we will cut off your bank accounts."

Gayle stared. The final line was delivered with no small amount of poorly hidden triumph. As if they thought they had one over on her.

She laughed, setting down the soup spoon and rising from the table. "Oh, poorly played, Father," she said, chuckling. "So, if you cut off the bank accounts, then I really *will* have an incentive to stay in the Academy—I'll be broke. I guess I'll tell them to start sending me the stipend." Gayle picked up her wine glass, now thoroughly in the mood for a drink. "Thanks, guys. I was having a bad week and this was just the bit of entertainment I needed to lift my spirits."

Her father rose as well, face drawn tight. "You're a High Tier woman. You've never lived on your own, with nothing. You think you'd survive, but you wouldn't. People inured to luxury never adjust well to the lack of it."

"I have friends."

Father sneered, before he caught himself and smoothed the ill-bred expression from his face. "I'm aware of your friends. And the male."

Gayle's eyes narrowed. "Ithann? Well, I can't marry anyway. There's a clause in the contract that I have to remain available for a Yadeshi warrior to choose until I've completed training and been assigned or released."

Miranda waved a hand. "That contract won't be a problem to get you out of." Her mother smiled, placidly. "Shall we start interviewing designers for your gown? I think a wedding next spring is a reasonable amount of time to prepare. And it gives you time to pick your pet charity project as a married woman."

Gayle expected that kind of frothiness from her mother, who made playing dumb an art—the perfect politician's wife who hid her intelligence and individuality under a layer of makeup and a pound of permanently inserted weave. At least Gayle's braids were all her own hair.

"I just don't understand how we can live in the twenty-second century and a woman's only value to her family is still directly correlated to the wealth of the man she snags to marry."

"Just a High Tier woman," her father said, stony. "Low and Middle Tier women have made advances in science and business. Unfortunately, the cost of being raised a spoiled rich brat is that you are expected to conform to outdated gender norms—to protect the wealth that sheltered you from food and educational deprivation."

They stared at each other. "I'm not getting married, Father."

"Two weeks, Abigail. That's how long you have to resign yourself to your real life."

* * *

Gayle spent the rest of the evening in her room. She began to catalogue her belongings to see which items she owned outright and could sell, and which were family heirlooms she could smuggle out when she left. She raided the wine cellar for a bottle of the good stuff, of course, before beginning her inventory. It took some effort to quietly move around her available funds without tripping off any alerts her father might have had on her accounts, but the more wine she drank, the more fun the virtual shenanigans became.

Browsing the internet for inexpensive studio apartments, a new thought occurred to her and she set the thought of an efficiency aside, instead spending some time pouring over the paperwork she'd signed when admitted to YETI. After filing a few more documents, she leaned back in her chair with a smirk. Her father planned, and she planned. And she was the best of planners.

But if that plan fell through, then technically she could qualify for a housing voucher. Children of rich families weren't automatically assigned the same Tier of their parents unless they had money in their own name. Gayle had the stipend she'd been refusing from the Academy every month. And a small mutual fund every month that was her inheritance from a grandparent. Father couldn't touch that. Along with whatever loose credits she could stash, Gayle had just enough to get a few months' down payment on a place until her housing application was processed, and she was placed on a work waiting list.

Gayle grinned, wondering what in the hell the case workers could do with her file. Her education was appropriately eclectic for her social status—in other words, useless for most normal positions.

She was high enough ranked in her training group that she could request a room in the Academy—but Mother was right. Gayle would feel bad about taking accommodations away from a person who had no other options. She could manage on her own, it would just be an adjustment. Gayle had known this was coming for a while, so she had already prepared herself mentally.

Her communication console chimed. "Accept, hologram," she said.

A hologram-sized Mila appeared at the end of Gayle's bed.

"Hey, girl. I need your help with something."

"Will it be boring?"

"Absolutely not."

"Will it piss my father off?"

Mila grinned. "Hell, yeah, it will."

Gayle swung off her bed, setting aside her glass. "I'm in."

Download at
Emmaalisyn.com/warriorsmate

ABOUT THE AUTHOR

Emma Alisyn writes paranormal romance because teaching high school biology wasn't like how it is on television. Her lions, tigers, and bears will most interest readers who like their alphas strong, protective and smokin' hot; their heroines feisty, brainy and bootilicious; and their stories with lots of chemistry, tension and plenty of tender moments.